COMING SOON
FROM
JINGAWORKS

-JINGA
  A CAPOEIRA TALE

-CITY OF PALMS

-FREEPASS

-AVA

www.jingaworks.com

www.myspace.com/jingaworks

SPITTIN' GAME

A NOVEL

T. L.

BRYANT

JINGAWORKS

www.jingaworks.com

www.myspace.com/jingaworks

PUBLISHED BY JINGAWORKS

The cataloging-in-publication data is on file with the Library of Congress.

ISBN-978-0-615-26273-4

Printed in the United States of America

For Connie-

May God's loving eternal arms wrap around you
wherever you go because I know where God leads
me; you are there.

For Kai-

My warrior princess

My all

Mi vida

All I am and all I do is for you.

I love you!

<u>Acknowledgements</u>

First and foremost thank you to my
Heavenly Father for the gift of expression and
creativity; for your continuous patience and
forgiveness for the dumb stuff I get myself into.
With you Lord Jesus, I know all things are possible.

A big thanks to Kai, my inspiration for
everything I do in my life. I love you, baby.

A huge thanks to the Guilty Parties, whose
names have been changed to protect the innocent
(and to keep them from suing my black ass).

Rene' for the love through the years, you
helped make me the man I am. I will always cherish
you and everything you have given me in my life.

Big Dex, thanks for all the advice, all the
nights at the spot spittin' game, reading the
chapters, and just for you being you. You helped me

get through some rough times and helped me stay focused; I love you Bro.

A big thanks to Carmela, for inspiring me, making me believe in my talent, and just overall loving me. You're more than just a dime; you're a diamond.

Thank you to Ms Chris for editing and positive friendship.

Thank you to Mike J for checkin' out the rough draft, and all the funny conversation.

Thank you to Mom and Pop for everything you've given me especially love and ambition. I hope that you're not blushing too bad reading this book.

Thank you to Ms. Palmer for the advice about the literary world.

Thank you Adele Brinkley for Editing and advice.

Thanks to Airyka for the Editing and advice.

Thank you Rich Normandin for the work on the cover.

Thank you to Lulu Publishing for creating a place for me to self publish.

And Most of all thank you for buying this book…unless your cheap ass rented this from the library or stole it or something then to hell with you! I'm just playin', however you got it, thank you for taking the time out of your life to read the words of mine.

-T. L. Bryant

THE GAME

x

XAVIER

Man, I do it all for the nookie, and the nookie is thoroughly kickin' my ass. Damn! I can't believe what a playa's gotta go through! I swear I'm through with the game! I'm done! It's six-thirty in the morning, I ain't had no sleep, and I'm on my way to the bar. My brother Michael wakes me up at six in the morning, yeah let me back up; six in the morning in late October, in the freakin' Midwest, not California, naw, not Florida, hell no, in Indianapolis, which means its cold as penguin shit on a glacier out here right now.

Anyway, he tells me and Kyle, our other brother, to meet him at Rosa's, this bar and grill on 10th and Shadeland. Michael's the oldest, Kyle's the youngest, and yes you guessed it, I'm the middle brother, as in always in the middle of some shit that they done got into! All I know is somebody better be dead, pregnant, or both after the night I had, but we'll get back to that later. Ah here's the spot …

As I pull into the parking lot of Rosa's Bar and Grill, I see my boy Chuck, the owner, sweeping out front with that crusty old burnt cigar in his mouth and crumpled up derby on his head and looking like Fred Sanford on a bender. Chuck's cool though. He was like Dolomite, Redd Foxx, and Yoda wrapped into a little, seventy-year-old body. As he was preparing to open for the breakfast crowd, I'm hoping he could give me a head's up on Mike.

"Hey, man what's up?" I shake Chuck's hand.

"I don't know, Youngblood. Man, what is up with you and that bag? You remind me of that boy in Charlie Brown with the damn dirty ass, dusty blanket."

Clutching my backpack, I roll my eyes. "Don't worry about it. What's up with Mike?"

Chuck wraps his hands around the broomstick, leaning against it, "I don't know. He was sittin' on the curb when I came in to open. I felt sorry for him. He looked like he lost his dick in a bad poker hand. I didn't wanna leave him out there. He went inside, grabbed a bottle of Jack, put a fifty on the bar, and sat in the corner. He ain't said a single word except to call you and Kyle. He just looks like refried shit. Man, go talk to him; he can't have people seeing him like this."

"A'ight, Chuck, good looking out." I pat Chuck on the back and head to Michael's table. My heart is racing seeing Mike this way. Curiosity tightens my nerves. I feel my right eyebrow rise at the sight of Mike with his head hung low and looking like a kid with his hand stuck in an empty cookie jar. A large black pinstriped fedora casts a shadow of shame over his face as I sit and subtly sliding the bottle away from him.

"A'ight man, I'm here, what's up?" I pull up my chair.

Michael looks up slightly and says, "You and that damn bag."

"Don't worry about my bag, what's up?"

Michael sips from the shot glass, "I'm out. It's over."

"What are you talking about?"

"I'm done. I'm dropping out of the race."

"What!? We're two damn weeks from Election Day and tomorrow is the Urban Christian League Rally. Once we get their support, the election is a lock! You're this close to being the next Congressman in this district. Why would you drop out now?"

"Dude, last night I got myself in some shit."

"What'd you do?"

"Man …"

"Aw shit … Am I gonna have to beat your ass? What did you do, Michael?"

Michael throws back the entire shot glass, "Man, you ain't gonna believe this shit."

"Try me."

CHAPTER ONE

MAN PANTIES
MICHAEL

"Xavier, you know Debra has been bitchin' about only being able to spend time with the 'Future Congressman Thompson' and not being able to spend time with 'Big Mike'?"

"Yeah okay?"

"Yesterday I told her we'll spend the night at that bed and breakfast on the Northside."

"What, the Nasty Kitty?"

"No dumbass, the other one. You know Passions?"

"Yeah, yeah, I've heard of it. That's suppose to be a real nice little spot. Went up there to get your freak on, put her legs behind her head huh?"

Michael pours another drink, "Yeah, well I told ol' girl to get her hair done, get a nice dress, and I'll call and set everything up. So, I got to the spot and laid out rose petals on the bed and floor. I had the incense and oils on the nightstand, champagne chilling in the fridge, candles lit, with a little Teddy Pendergrass on the stereo. Man I was ready to beat it up like Holyfield in the twelfth."

"Damn! Sounds good so far."

"Well hold on …"

It was a nice night, cold fall wind blowing, the moon was high and full and I was ready for a night of hot sex. After all, since the campaign it has been a while since we got down. So we did the bubble bath thang, sipped on some Dom, had a few imported French chocolates. Then we toweled off and went to the bedroom.

Now on the bed, I'm going down on her like a fat kid on Krispy Kreme and she was into it, but not all the way. You know she wasn't *there*, you know *there*, yet? So I asked her, "What's up?"

Debra sat up in the bed and sighed, "Well … the flowers, candy, bubble bath they are all nice but Baby this is the same routine, just in a different place. I wanna do something … a little freaky, you know a little adventurous."

I continued to make soft kisses on her inner thighs, "Well what do you want Baby? Anything, all you got to do is ask."

Debra got up from the bed and walked over to the closet. "How bout a little role-play?"

Debra pulled out these two white garment bags. She unzipped the first bag and took out some pink lace lingerie, high heel boots, a garter belt, and a pair of silk panties.

I sat down on the bed feeling my lips part a wide smile. "Oh yeah, I like this. This is good, this is real good," I said rubbing my hands together.

Then Debra opened the second bag and pulled out a three quarter length black pen stripe suit, black gators, complete with a laid out sharp ass fedora hat. I had to admit, this suit was bad! Nothing makes a man feel like a man more than a well-draped suit. I walked over to the closet and slid my hand across the suit, admiring the smooth fabric.

"Damn, this shit is on point," I said. "This is a bad ass ebony man of the millennium, Billy Dee Williams, meets Tony Montana pimp suit! This shit is tight! So, what we gonna do, play the pimp and naughty ho' who's fifty dollars short? Cool! Yeah Baby I can do a little role-playing."

My cell phone rang, "Oh damn, it's Xavier. I'll be right back, Baby. Why don't you slip into that little outfit, and I'll go into the bathroom and get rid of him."

"A'ight Baby. Hurry up," Debra grabbed my neck pulling me close. Her soft, red stained lips against mine, made my nerves tremble. I forced myself away to jog into the bathroom.

"Hey X, what's up?"

"Hey man, I just wanted to remind you that we are meeting at Campaign Headquarters to go over your speech to the Urban Christian League on Saturday. Don't forget, man. We need those votes so that speech is gotta be on point. Afterwards, we're having the town hall meeting with the youth voters on campus at I.U.P.U.I. So, Saturday is gonna be a major day."

"All right, man, I got it. X, I'm about rock this girl's world! I have got to show you this phat suit she got me, straight out of G.Q. You gonna love it, Dude! I'll see you tomorrow, I'm about to knock one outta the park! Later."

I turned off the phone, reached in my small leather bag, and pulled out a bottle of cologne. Splashing on a few drops, I looked in the mirror, brushed my eyebrows, and mustache with my fingers. With a wink at myself, I headed back into the bedroom to give this girl the night of her life! I opened the bathroom door and got ready to walk into paradise.

"All right Baby, I hope you ready for this big dick ... what the fuc ... ?" I couldn't believe this shit! I dropped my bag in shock as I eyed Debra up and down: She was wearing the freakin' men's suit, hat, and shoes!

"Wh ... what are you doing?"

"I said I wanted to do something a little different."

"So what, you got another suit in the closet?"

"No," She giggles.

"So ... what the hell am I suppose to put on?"

Debra's eyes motioned to the lingerie. My eyes got wide as all outdoors!

"Oh hell naw!" I protested.

"Come on baby, come on. Just play along. I was talking to one of the girls in my yoga class ... ."

"Hell, no!"

"She said her and her man do role reversal all the time."

"I don't give a damn!"

"But Mike."

"No! No! No! I am not wearin' this shit! Next thing you know you want to put on a strap on and screw me in the ass!"

Her eyes motioned away as a dildo dropped from behind her back.

"Oh hell naw! Naw! We might as well pack this shit up and go right now! I'll get the car, shit!" I got my overnight bag. "Shoot, you must be crazy."

"Wait Baby, wait." She walks over to me. "I'm just playin' with you, I would never do anything that would hurt you. But come on let's do something freaky."

Debra unhooked a pair of underwear from the hanger, "Why do you just put these on as a compromise?"

"You want me to put on some pink lace panties? Are you insane?"

"Come on, besides these are not panties. They're French Silk Bloomers."

I grabbed the underwear, "Bullshit! These are some Frenchie Man Panties at best! I am not puttin' this shit on. No!"

"Come on, Baby, I'll do that thing you like." Debra fell into a full split, grinding the ground as if she was riding me. She eyed me up and down seductively, tracing an outline of her body with the panties. She slowly dragged it across her chest, moaning deeply. "Hmmm Big Daddy, I want feel this silk against my wet walls. Put it on for Miss Kitty. Please?"

I rubbed my chest looking at Debra holding the underwear with that seductive smile. Usually, I loved that damn look, but now it was different. Now, I'm being conned like a New York mark. "Damn, why you gotta go there? Man, shit, are you for real?"

"Yeah, boy, put these on for me. Please."

"N...n...n...no! I ain't doing this! You could have asked me to dress up as a clown, do a sexy dance, fry bacon butt naked, but this shit is too much!"

"Come on, I've been doing coochie crunches."

I sucked in as much air as I could, my dick got so hard it was particularly pointing right at the punanny, "Hmmm, coochie crunches?"

"Boy, I can crack a walnut in this coochie."

"Damn! For real?"

"I'll milk you dry and have you limpin' for a week," she said, dangling those damn panties on her index finger.

Rubbin' my crotch, I thought about it for a minute. "Shit, you better not tell nobody about this," I said snatching the draws to put them on.
"Shit, I do kinda like the way they feel against my skin. A'ight, bring yo sexy ass here!"

"Hmmmm." She pulled a bobby pin from her hair.

At that point, I picked Debra up and carried her to the bed. She looked so sexy in that damn suit, like she was ready to run thangs. Shit she had me in a pair of panties, so what does that tell you? I have to admit, I always liked a chick in power. Even though I felt like the ebony bitch of the week in these damn draws, I still had to show her I was ready to handle mine. I slipped off her suit pants over her Black gators. Her perfectly trimmed velvet womanhood

called me to her, and believe me, I had to answer. I
buried my face in the moist softness of her and took
every ounce of her sweetness in my mouth.

After fifteen minutes, I had my fill and could
tell she was ready to accept me. I pulled back my
panties; damn I hate the sound of that shit. Anyway, I
pulled them off to the side and enjoyed the bliss of
my beautiful wife. Her eyes rolled in the back of her
head and within moments we became lost in passion.
I rubbed her soft, smooth thighs as I felt the flicker of
my eyelids over my eyes going in the back of my
head.

Time and ecstasy become one as I glanced at
the clock and noticed an hour had passed. I slid my
hands behind the back of her knees and placed her
legs behind her head. I raised up and saw my baby,
suit tie and all with her feet hooked behind her head.
Looking down at her, I almost lost it right then and
there.

"Harder baby! Yeah! Get it!", she
screamed. The bed shook faster, banging against the
wall. She unhooked her legs to wrap them around me
like a wrestler ready to pin me down for the count.
Her legs and arms pulled me into her as far as she
could as we twisted and turned between the sheets.

"I'm cumming … Oh God, I'm cumming!!"
She screamed to the top of her lungs stretching her
legs to their limits. The next thing I knew the smoke
alarm goes off! I looked down at the floor and
noticed that Debra's foot accidentally knocked over
the oil lamp on the nightstand, igniting a fire
accelerated by the broken bottle of cologne pouring
out of my bag all over the floor. The flames shot up
like a rocket across the floor and up the curtains.
Within moments, smoke filled in the room. We
jumped out of bed panicked by the smoke alarm
screeching.

"Oh shit, come on!" I screamed grabbing my
robe. Debra puts on her robe and dashes out of the
suite. I grabbed my attaché case near the door and
followed her outside.

We ran across the hotel yard. The cold, wet
leaves over the grass numbed my feet, but I was
grateful just to be alive and have her safe with me.
We watched flames rise from the windows of our
room. Fire trucks and police Sirens wailed around the
complex as we held each other watching the fire and
people starting to gather outside the hotel.

"It's chilly out here." Debra said shivering, snuggling closer to me.

"I have a blanket in the car, I'll go get it."

"No, stay with me, I'll be okay."

"Come on we'll go to the get the blanket out the trunk."

We made our way to the car, huddling together from the cold fall air.

A news van pull up besides us, "Mr. Thompson! Mr. Thompson!" A voice yelled from the van. "Mr. Thompson, one moment please." A beautiful caramel-skinned honey stepped out with pad and tape recorder in hand and a cameraman close behind.

"Mr. Thompson! Mr. Thompson?! Is that you? Are you okay? Theresa Gomez, Inside Scoop. What happened here? Can you give us a statement?"

"Well, Miss Gomez, it looks like a small fire started in our room, but it appears that everyone is out and safe. Ah, there is Fire Inspector Peter Johnson. I'm sure he can better answer … ."

Suddenly, smoke poured from my attaché case, seconds later the bottom of my robe catches fire. I started screaming like a heifer in heat trying to put the fire out, but the wind was blowing fanning the flames higher.

"Take it off, Baby! Hurry up! Hurry!" Debra screamed trying to remove the robe. Theresa dropped her microphone trying to pat out the fire. I stumbled back and frantically ripped the robe off. I knew I was in some shit when I heard a simultaneous gasp followed by silence. Theresa covered her mouth at the sight of me dressed in pink silk panties, complete with ruffles, and a matching garter belt. Her cameraman's mouth dropped as he instinctively panned up and down. Debra looked around for something to cover me. My mouth crashed to the ground and quivered. I tried trying to say something, but I couldn't speak. All I could see is the red light from the camera recording.

Theresa snickered, "Uh…why don't we…uh…talk…to…um…Inspector…uh… Johnson. Come…Oh…God…come on, Jerry. Let's get an interview." Theresa walked to the hotel courtyard as Jerry gave me a freakish up and down look. I could only imagine what this Dude had to say. Jerry shook his head in disappointment, as if I just embarrassed every Black man in America.

"Damn, Dude." Jerry whispered.

"But brotha, you know how it is … ." I said with a stupid, shameful half smile.

"Naw, bro. I don't know nothin' about this shit you do, man. Damn!"

Only thing I could do was drop my head as Jerry rejoined Theresa.

Back at Rosa's, I listen in shock to Michael's account of last night. I got tears in my eyes trying to keep from laughing.

"So … so … so … ." I laugh hysterically. "What … what no … oh boy! Only you! Damn, Dude!"

"I know, shit! So you know how these damn tabloid reporters are, always looking for the story behind the story. Low and behold this morning I saw a commercial for a *special* expose' on my life on Inside Scoop. You know what that means, my career is jacked up, down the drain over a freakin' pair of panties, Man!" Michael slams his fist into the table. "This shit ain't funny, man. What am I gonna do?"

"Damn." I grab a shot glass and begin to pour a glass. Kyle walks in the bar. He nods at Chuck and sits down with us.

"What's crackin'!" He says picking up the bottle. "Jack, the breakfast of champions. A'ight, who got some bad pussy?"

"We gotta get that tape back. Pure and simple," I say.

"What tape?" Kyle asks.

"How are we gonna do it? You know Theresa ain't gonna give up the story."

"What tape? What are you talking about? What happened?" Kyle demands.

Michael raises the brim of his hat, "Man, where the hell have you been, Kyle?"

"Dude, I just got out of the lockup."

"What!" Michael and I exclaim.

"You mean the lockup as in jail?" Michael confirms.

"Yep, man I just got out." Kyle nonchalantly picking up a menu.

"How come you didn't call me?" I frown.

"Cause it was your fault I was there!"

I push down Kyle's menu. "Wait, slow down and start from the beginning. What the hell are you talking about, Kyle?"

CHAPTER TWO

SAUCY'S BIG PAYBACK

KYLE

Kyle shakes his head and looks out the window. "Xavier, do you remember Vanessa?"

"Your roommate?" I ask.

"Yeah. Mike, I don't think you met her yet?"

"No, I don't think so." Michael says rubbing the bottle.

"All this started two weeks ago … ."

I was flipping through the pages of my Economics book on the couch in my apartment. My mind went numb reading through the mundane pages. I closed my eyes and leaned my head back wishing I was anywhere but there. I started to chew on my pencil, thinking about a beach in Cancun when a door opened in the back of the apartment. I figured my roommate Vanessa was coming out to take a break from studying for her Chemistry mid-term. Vanessa was real cool, I'd known her for about five years. We met in high school; she was always real brainy and skinny as a twig off a dead tree. All changed last year. She started working at the Chinese Buffet on campus and got thicker than a brick. I mean she got ass, hips, and tits and can order Kung Pao Chicken in four languages.

Nonetheless, my Cancun, Tom Collins fantasy was interrupted by the sound of a Pepsi being cracked open and fizzing to the counter. I opened my eyes and felt my heart drop at the sight of Vanessa wiping up the countertop in just a bra and a pair of panties. Her titties jiggling back and forth while she cleaned the countertop was driving me crazy. Her statuesque, silky mocha frame seemed to be the perfect complement to the sun peering through the window blinds.

"Hey, babe, you want something out of here?" she called out. She turned around and knelt down to search in the fridge for a snack. I rubbed my thighs, the book dropped to my lap watching her slide her thumb across the brim of her panties to smooth her underwear over her ass. Leaning forward, I scraped the bottom of my lip across my front teeth. I pulled in my lips, just wanting time to stop for a moment, even just for a minute, just long enough to taste one fantasy, to quench one desire.

"Damn, Vanessa. What is that, an invitation for some or what?"

She put her hand on her hip and closed the fridge. "What?", she smiled innocently.

"Girl you can't be coming out in here showing a hungry brotha a full plate. I get confused."

Vanessa smiled and slowly walked over to me. She leaned down and for a second I thought she was gonna put it on me. My bubble burst when she reached over to kiss me on the forehead. I was trying to play it cool as Vanessa's heaving breasts seemingly bloomed in my face. I couldn't believe this flat-chested girl got these mountains from eating Egg Drop Soup and Moo Shu Pork!

She took another sip of her soda, "I just like being comfortable in my place. Besides, you know you my homey. I feel relaxed, like I can be myself in front of you, like you one of my girls. I'll see ya." She turned around to walk down the hallway. All I could do was bite my bottom lip and shake my head, staring at the thick luscious form sashaying away from me.

"You keep on walkin' around here like that, and I'm gonna show you a big ass difference between me and yo girls."

"Boy, you are so silly. I gotta get to class." She looked over her shoulder, smiled at me, and closed the door to her bedroom.

"Looking like two spiral hams in a slingshot, damn she got a lot of ass," I said to myself, sittin' back on the couch, looking up at the ceiling, as dumbfounded as a deer in the beams of a damn semi truck. I mean this shit's been going on for four months now. It's so bad that if I close my eyes take a deep breath, the air is still scented with the smell of her perfume, with a hint of cocoa butter. Damn, I wanted to hit, but there were a couple of problems. One she's a lesbian and two her gargaratan, truck-stop reject, bitch ass girlfriend could probably whoop my skinny ass. Nevertheless, damn she still got a lot of junk back there.

So later that night, I was waiting outside the Liberal Arts Building on Campus, blowing warm air into my hands, watching people head back and forth to their classes. My mind was still jacked up thinking about Vanessa and those long legs making that slow walk back to her room. I swear every step was a tease, every bounce a temptation. I ain't never been so close but just that far away. Fortunately, Xavier pulled up in his truck.

"Hey little Bro. You ready?"

"Hey, Xavier. Mike coming to eat with us?"

"Naw, he's got the flu. He's probably is overworked from the campaign. I know he'll be happy when this is over."

"I know. Debra too, but you gotta give him props, two years ago it was just me, you, and Mike in Johnny's Barber Shop spittin' game about the honeys, bullshittin' about politics."

"I know. Who would have thought he would have taken that shit so seriously. I'm proud of him though."

"Yeah, me too, Dude. He really came up."

Xavier drove his truck out of the parking lot. "You look like you have something on your mind."

"Aw shit, man, I'm 'bout to bust, I can't take this shit no more."

"Vanessa still walkin' around in her draws?"

"Hell yeah! This is some bull!"

Xavier laughed, "Man, you a better one than me. Women always do that shit; they don't even be thinking nothin' of it. I had a girl do that shit all the time, walk around the house butt-naked. But then let me ask for some, and it was always, 'all you think about is sex. Is that all I am to you, some pussy on tap? Well, shit, you the one walking out here with you na-nas and yum-yum showin'. What do you expect me to do? Let me pull out a couple of first class tickets to Paris and lay them on her nightstand. Dammit, you gonna think we about to hop our asses on a plane. But let me say is that all I am to you is a free trip, and I'm guess what … .''

"Cut off!" we said, simultaneously making scissors motions with our fingers.

"Man, I do have to give it to you because if it was me, we wouldn't be friends. You know what I would do?''

"What, man?''

"I would go to the store and get four things. A bottle of baby oil, a half-gallon of chocolate milk, a little baby T-shirt that's like three sizes too small, and a porno tape.''

"Okay …'' I giggled.

Xavier leaned to the side in the driver's seat stroking his chin. I knew he was about to come up with some shit.

"I would wait until Vanessa came home and would be there for a while. Then I'd go in my room and lock the door, take off all my clothes; I mean everything, draws and all. Then I would take the baby oil, grease my whole body up, and put in the porno, but I wouldn't jack off. I'd just get it nice and hard. I mean hard with one of those Viraga-laden, battleship, slay all beasts, erections. You know one of those hard ones you can put a hole through the wall with?! I'm talking about pogo stick, pole vault, four in morning and ain't peed yet, Sir Lancelot hard ons."

I leaned against the dashboard and cracked up laughing, "Dude, you crazy."

"Oh I ain't done! Then I would take the little baby T-Shirt, put it on, and walk out just like that, dick swinging in the wind. I'd go straight to the fridge and crack open the chocolate milk, take a big ass swig, let the milk pour down the front of my shirt, get it all wet and milky. Then I'd turn around like Mandingo in bloom and ask Vanessa if she wanted something out of here. When she asks what I'm doing. I'd tell her that I'm just getting comfortable, hope you don't mind. I'd walk around for the rest of the day like that too, with my dick out. I'd be opening curtains, dialing the phone, and fluffin' pillows with it. I'd sit right there on the couch doing homework with my dick out. I'd use my Johnson as a damn bookstand. I'd turn around and 'look no hands' smack her in the ass with it."

I was in snitches, "You silly man. You know what, I'm gonna do it."

Xavier laughed. "What?"

"I'm gonna do what you just said."

"What?"

"I'm gonna do the thing with the oil, porno, and the milk."

Laughing, Xavier put on his turn signal. "Yeah, right!"

"I'm serious."

"Whatever, Dude."

"Man, I'm for real."

"I got fifty that says you won't do it."

"I got a hundred that says I do."

"A'ight, cool a hundred."

"A'ight."

Now, yesterday I was in my bedroom typing an Economics report. I was focused on facts, figures, and theories when I heard the front door open and shut. I walked to the bedroom door and peeked out to see Vanessa sitting down on the couch on the phone. I closed my eyes and thought for a minute; I nodded my head 'yes' and quietly closed and locked the door. My pulse quickened at the thought of the covert mission ahead in the name of all teased men. I dimmed the lights and rubbed my hands together, smiling as I opened my top dresser drawer. I pulled back my underwear and took out the porno tape I bought just for this occasion. I cracked open the case and held the tape up to the small light on the dresser.

Booty Meat, "This should do the trick," I said to myself with a devilish grin as I put the tape in the VCR. I took off my clothes and put on the baby T-shirt I borrowed from Vanessa's closet. A minute later, I turned on the T.V. and put the volume on mute. As lights flickered from the television, I had to grip the remote tightly to keep from spanking off. The room seemed to get hotter by the second; sweat began to bead on my forehead, neck, and chest.

I was at full attention, ready to take on the world. I opened one of the three bottles of baby oil and rubbed the oil all over my body, tingling from the erotic images on the T.V.

Twenty-five minutes passed, and it was time. I turned off the T.V. and poured on the other two bottles of oil.

"Showtime." I whispered, looking down at my swollen, greasy, throbbing shaft. I thumped it with my middle finger and thumb, "We about show this girl something Lil K!" I whispered tiptoeing over to the bedroom door. I opened it and noticed Vanessa laughing, still on the phone sitting on the couch with her back turned to me. I slipped out of the room and crept over into the kitchen. Every nerve in my body was alive and craving sweet revenge.

I slowly opened the refrigerator door and knelt down to get the chocolate milk. I rubbed my slippery hand on my shirt, grabbed the half-gallon of chocolate milk, and closed my eyes bringing the jug to my lips. I took a huge gulp, letting the milk flow over my body like a river splashing over rocks in at the bottom of a waterfall. With my shirt completely saturated, I turned around, chest bulging, muscles flexed, and with a chocolate milk moustache smile that stretched from ear to ear, I spun around to give Vanessa the midnight, red light special show. I licked my lips and in my deepest, sexiest voice I said, "Hey, Baby, you want some of this?"

Right when I said that, Vanessa's father, Fred, steps out of the bathroom. I was in absolute freakin' shock. My dick went from mighty battleship to a wet dishrag in seconds. I gotta think of something to say to this 6'5, 365 lbs. massive dude staring at me, but I'm frozen solid. My heart pounded so hard it was like it was trying to jump out my chest and escape from the baby tee shirt. My hands quivered, sending the milk splashing like a powerful orgasm. Everything after that happened in super slow motion. Fred's face tightened like a hardened Marine, his neck budged causing the priest collar around his neck to pop and split in two. Vanessa looked up at her father and turned around. Her mouth dropped, the phone followed.

Fred yanked off his suit jacket. "Negro, what you doing with your dick out in front of my baby girl?! What the hell is gonna on up in here?"

"Uh … uh … uh … uh … Ma … Ma … Mr. Rich … ." I stammered trying to dig deep to find the words to get out of this situation that seemed like such a good idea before the Black Loc Ness Monster showed up.

As if that wasn't bad enough, "What is going on out here?" Barbara, Vanessa's mother, walked out of Vanessa's room. She dropped the drink in her hand. "Kyle!" she screamed in surprise. "...Oh Kyle." She smiled looking down in brief admiration. I was feeling good for a millisecond, but I think that fact that his wife was now looking at my dick made Fred really pissed. Barbara quickly came out of her daze to see Fred grinding his teeth and panting like a colossal bull staring at a matador wrapped in a red sheet. I felt the rage steaming off Fred's baldhead.

"Baby ... Baby calm down. Baby .... Baby?" Barbara stepped toward Fred grabbing his arm. He wasn't havin' it. He quickly snatched it back

"Naw ... Naw ... NAW!! Oh, HELL NO! Lord, give me strength, ten feet, and a good lawyer! I got to beat yo ass, ain't no way around that! I got to! Come here!"

Somehow, I just knew I was in deep shit at this point. Barbara was trying to hold him back from rushing to the kitchen, but he couldn't be stopped. I was about to piss on myself and Vanessa's ass was just stuck there, looking in shock at the scene in front of her.

Fred hurdled over the loveseat, and my adrenaline must have skyrocketed because I knew I had to get out of Dodge. I tried to get back to the bedroom, but the damn floor was so covered in milk I slipped and fell on my ass. I tried to crawl to the room, but and I felt his claw on my back. Fred grabbed on to me, I'm screaming like a ho on payday, but my ass is so slick that I kept slipping out of his hands.

The next thing I knew, Fred's big ass slipped and slid into the bedroom door, knocking it off the hinges. Now he was real pissed because his eyes were devil red, full of fire. He got ready to make another pass, but I scurried my ass off the floor and dashed to the nearest door available. Only problem was, it was the damn front door! So there I was, out the apartment with my junk out for all to see. This ain't good, I didn't even have time to turn around cause Fred was on my ass. I was slippin' and slidin' down the apartment hallway, like I'm surfing barefoot with Fred still clawing at me.

I tried to zigzag down the hallway, but with every turn Fred was just catching up; his bloodshot eyes fueling my retreat. I looked in the distance and saw daylight. Thank God! I kicked it into high gear and crashed through the front door of the apartment building. I reached back to slam the door and knocked over a few garbage cans, hoping to buy a few seconds.

Back at Rosa's Kyle holds his head in his hands as Michael and I die laughing on the floor. I choke trying to take a drink of water, "Oh shit…Oh shit, Dude! This is too good. I don't believe this shit. So then what?"

"So I'm outside … "

I was lookin' to the left, the right, sideways for somebody I knew, a car to jump into, a bush or somethin' shit! Not only that but classes were out, so everybody is outside to see "Slicky Dicky" run through the streets. Everybody's laughing their asses off, lovin' this shit.

Next thing I knew the apartment building doors explode open, off the hinges, and Fred was on my ass like a horse at the Kentucky Derby. I swear to God, he jumped over the nine, ten freakin' stairs to the street! This big dude was airborne, and he wasn't missing a step. He came down there like he just got out of bed! So did the only thing I could do.

"You squared off and clocked his ass?" Michael retorts.

"Hell naw, fool I ran. You crazy! Are you paying attention?" I took off down the street like a freed slave with Vanessa's daddy tight on my ass. I can't shake him. He ain't out of breath, he ain't sweatin,' he was just mad! I'm so scared I felt my heart beating in my balls! I'm runnin' through traffic, bobbin' and weaving, knocking down garbage cans. I was screaming down the street, lookin' behind me to see if he was still there, and BAM I ran right into a fucking Campus Police Officer. The cop was on a bike, I knocked him off of that, the coffee that he was holding spilled on Fred, burning him, so he's rolling around on the ground holding his face, and there I was on top of the cop. My dick was on his face covered in baby oil, and he was pissed beyond pissativity!

"Damn! Man, what the hell? Did he take you both to jail?" I laugh.

"Naw, Xavier. He took Fred to the hospital and wrapped a beach towel around me and swept me off to the county jail."

"Well at least you got the bulldog off your ass."

"Oh, no then I get to the lockup!"

"Aw, shit what happened there?"

"You ever see feeding time at the lion's den at the zoo? I might as well have been a side of beef with a booty hole."

The cop put a towel around my waist and put me in handcuffs. The ride to the county jail was pretty short, I guess since I'd smacked this cop in the mouth with my dick he probably wanted to get me to holding A.S.A.P. before he did something he would regret. I was booked and escorted over to the holding area. I felt my knees crack as I made the long, slow trip to the cell. This was the first time I'd been in any type of trouble so I was petrified. But I knew I had to man up, can't be no punk. I tried to swallow, but nothing would relieve the lump in my throat. The smell of semen and urine choked the air. I tried not to make eye contact with anyone just like I tried to block out the stench. I felt eyes following me like lights guiding a night flight off the runway.

The cell door opened; the menacing sound of the top of door sliding across the ceiling's groove was almost as scary as a rusty in chainsaw starting in a dark forest at midnight. I knew then this wasn't a bad dream; it was real. The cop nudged me on into the cell, and next thing I knew I hear the sound of the door slamming behind me, sealing my fate. This was some bullshit. Inside the cell, I felt more eyes on me, and some of those eyes were on my damn towel. I turned around and see three men staring at me. I don't know if it was because I looked scared beyond reason or if it was because I looked like the poster boy for ghetto prison sex. I grabbed on to the bars of the cell and heard footsteps behind me coming close. "Aw shit here we go." I thought as I felt the reek of shit-laced hot breath against the back of my neck followed by a heavy weight on my shoulder. I got my nuts up in case I needed to fire off on somebody. I moved my eyes over slightly to size up the owner of the hairy, greasy hand on me.

"What yo name is?"

I turned my back to him, "Hey, can I get a jumpsuit or something in here?" I screamed out to a cop.

"We'll get you something in a minute. We got some more people coming in," the guard said passing by my cell.

I felt another tap on my shoulder, "I said what your name is?"

I didn't answer; I was trying not to inhale shit face's breath. So this other dude steps up. "Naw, naw, naw, Bill. I know what his name is, look at his shirt."

Aw, shit I forgot. This can't get no fuckin' worse. I looked down at the shirt I borrowed from Vanessa. Of all the shirts in her closet, I got to take the one that says "SAUCY" spelled out in gold glittered sequence letters. I looked like a fucking 70's disco drag queen reject from a gay porno movie. Bill spun me around facing the back of the cell. My butt clinched tight enough to make a diamond out of a piece of coal.

"Good Lord! Saucy! Woo! Is it my birthday?" This freak screams from the back, sounding like Michael Jackson in a nutcracker. I guessed he was the bitch of the group … shit until now.

"Naw, Jimmy," Bill said. "This is my birthday gift."

Bill grabbed the cell bars close to me, staring me up and down and smacking his tar Black lips.

"Yeah…" Bill inhaled. His raspy voice was bringing up my lunch. "Saucy, huh? I like that. I bet you a Spicy truffle too, ain't ya, Saucy? I got something for dat Spicy ass, too." Bill sucks his teeth. "You all shiny and new like a fish out of water."

"Like a merman!!!" Jimmy cried from the back, rubbing on his skinny-ass chest.

"You got me all sweaty, give me that towel." Bill said running his hand across his stomach. "Let me show yo Spicy ass something."

"Look, Dude, I don't do that funny shit." I said slowly backing away looking for something to cold cock this fool with.

He slid back to me, "We gonna see how saucy dat ass is tonight when we get transferred." Bill raked this index finger across my stomach, then across his lips. His tongue glided across, wiping the oil off. "Hmmm, tasty."

I smiled and circled my index finger in and out of my belly button, looking Bill up and down. "You like that, uh?"

"Yeah, Saucy."

"Since you had one, it's my turn."

"What you want you, lil' saucy bitch? You wanna suck on this big dick, huh? I can always pick you little fishes out, can't I?"

"Sho' you right." Jimmy giggled.

"Hmm, let me get a taste." I said.

"Naw, fish, wait till tonig ... "

Before he could finish his thought, I grabbed that bastard's nuts like he stole em' from me. I dug my nails in and yanked hard toward the ground. Bill hunched over, and I blew him a kiss slamming my head into his stomach and instantly launched the top of my head into Bill's nose, the impact breaking it. Bill dropped to the ground. I was about ready to kick the shit out of him.

"Oh my! You just fierce Trojan, ain't you! Hmmph! I like that!" Jimmy cried from the back.

"Who else want some of Saucy? Damnit!" I yelled.

"Shit, I do!!!" Jimmy giggles.

A guard walked up to the cell. Looking down on Bill, he asked, "Is there a problem here?"

"No, Sir. I just slipped,", Bill said wiping off his nose.

"Good, then get yo big ass up then. Kyle Thompson!"

I turned around. "Here, Sir!"

"You made bail. Out!"

I had to give Kyle his props. I put my arm around his shoulder, "Well, man, I'm proud of you. When you ass was out, you ran, and when it was on line you whooped ass. What happened next?"

"Nessa bailed me out, and here I am. What a damn night, and Big Bro. you owe me one hundred dollars."

Michael gets up laughing, "Aw, damn, Dude I got to take a piss."

"Man, a deal's a deal, and I will say Dude you earned this," I pass Kyle a hundred dollar bill.

Kyle snaps the bill and kisses it. "So, X, why are we here, what's the big rush?"

"Long story short, our big brother got caught on tape in some panties."

"What? What you mean!"

"And of all people to see this shit, he was caught on tape by guess who?"

"Who?"

"Theresa Gomez"

Kyle's mouth drops, "What? Big Titty, Tattling, Tabloid, Theresa Gomez on the gossip show? Oh, shit, are you serious?"

"As Cancer," I reply.

"Damn! Well, we can't let him go out like that. What we gonna do?"

"We only got one choice, we have to get that tape back."

Michael returns to the table, "What ya'll talking about?"

I push out my chair. "We're getting your prancing panties tape back. Kyle and I are gonna go down to the studio to talk to Gomez. Why don't you get cleaned up, and we'll meet you back at your place. Stay off the phone and be low key until we can get the tape back"

"Man, she ain't gonna give it up." Michael says.

"We don't have much of a choice do we? We can't have you giving a speech in front of the Urban Christian League on Saturday and Friday night you on the eleven o' clock news shakin' you ass in a pair a panties and fishnets. What's that gonna say?"

"All right, so like I said, I don't have a choice but to drop out."

"That's bullshit, Dude. We have fought too hard to drop out a couple of weeks before the election; plus the community needs you. People are starting to believe that politicians can do something positive. Shit, Rex Manning has been fucking over the East Side for years. You're the first opponent in twenty years even to stand a chance against him, and we're what … two weeks away? No, man I can't let you do that." I sigh. "Don't worry about this right now. You just get ready to make that speech to the League tomorrow and let your little brothers handle this."

"A'ight, X, a'ight, a'ight. If ya'll can do it, fine. Get at me if you need something, and I'll be hiding out at the crib until I hear from you."

Kyle steps up and gives Michael a hug, "We got your back man. Just keep your *own* draws on."

"Amen, damnit!" I agree and hug Michael. Michael puts the cap back on the Jack bottle and waves to Chuck. Kyle and I pull down the brims of our baseball caps as we walk out of Rosa's like soldiers on a search and destroy mission. The bell over the front door at Rosa's chimes as we hit the pavement.

CHAPTER THREE

THE STORY

THERESA

"Miss Gomez, you have calls on lines one, three, five, and six."

"Thank you, Sarah."

I guess my little expose' is causing quite a stir. Well, that's no surprise. Rex Manning's camp has been calling all morning, trying to get the scoop on my special story about Michael Thompson.

"Excuse me, Miss Gomez."

I'm pushing the intercom button for what seems like the fiftieth time this hour, "Yes, Tim."

"We have another delivery from Mr. Manning's campaign headquarters."

"Bring it in."

Tim walks in holding a bouquet of three-dozen red roses and a bottle of Château Lafite Rothschild Pauillac. Somehow Manning found out I liked expensive wines and this one was real nice

1996 and about $300.00 a bottle. He has good taste
I'll give him that.

"Send it back, Tim. All of it, and tell Sarah to
take messages for the calls on hold. I need to get to
Editing."

"Yes, Miss Gomez." Tim says and closes the
door behind him.

Mr. Manning is trying to get at me like I was
the last virgin on prom night. I couldn't blame him
though. This election is the hottest story in Indy right
now. Rex Manning has been the Congressman on the
East Side for about the last twenty years and I've
never seen things so messed up. This guy is so bad he
could fuck up a cup of hot chocolate. Poverty rates
are the highest ever, crime rates have skyrocketed,
and voter turnout is down just his district while he
gets fat. He's a classic example of the huge political
machine keeping the status quo.

Manning's especially hot because there is a
huge revitalization effort scheduled to happen in his
district next spring. The city has issued a series of
high dollar contracts for rebuilding a massive part of
the East Side. Word is that Manning's got his hooks
in about three of the biggest construction firms in the
city. If Manning loses the election, he's gonna lose

the opportunity to get on the ground floor of all the juicy kickbacks from the multi-million dollar contracts. Thompson is the only real opponent Manning's ever had, and they couldn't be any more opposite. Manning wants neighborhoods utilized for high dollar condominiums. Because the target area is so close to the downtown shopping and art district, the area could be prime real estate if the city's proposal goes through. Thompson, on the other hand, wants to have the area rent protected if the revitalization goes through so that the people who live in those areas, mostly poor working class, aren't forced to move out. Manning's nervous and looking for any leverage, and here I am caught in the middle, which is just fine with me.

I'm walking to Editing when my boss, Mr. Dicklis, pulls me over. Trust me his name fits him perfectly.

"Good morning Theresa."

"Good morning, Sir."

"Heading over to Editing?"

"Yes, Sir. I have quite a bit of work to do with the Thompson story."

"Ah, yes, the Thompson story. Quite a popular piece, hmmm?"

"Well, I'm hoping, Sir." I smile, knowing this is the story of the year.

"You know this is a break for this station, an exclusive like this could make us a ratings giant in this demographic."

"I'm sure."

"Why don't I give you a hand with the story? An experienced mind might help you to put a solid spin on it."

"I think I'll be fine. Thank you, Sir."

"Perhaps I can watch you work. Maybe you can teach me something."

I crack a fake ass smile. "I'd like to, but we're pretty much have a full house in there."

"Miss Gomez, may I ask you a question?"

"Of course, Sir."

"Are we a team?"

"What?"

"Are we a team?"

"Sir, with all due respect I have a lot of work…"

"I asked you a question: are we a team?"

"Yes, Sir."

"So we want to do everything we can to make the team as strong as possible, right?"

"Of course, Sir."

He leans in to whisper to me, "Good, I glad to see we are on the same page. Now, because you are my best reporter, I'm going to let you in on a little secret. Mr. Manning has offered a very generous stipend to our station. I know that you do usually freelance work, but this could mean a lot to this station and to you: a new set for Inside Scoop, better equipment. You could go from covering local and state news to national, maybe international affairs. Big celebrity trials, scandals, I know you live for that sort of thing."

"And for this stipend, what would Mr. Manning like in return?" I ask as if I don't already know.

The coffee stained smile across his sour pink lips and pale face always made my skin crawl and still does as he puts his arm around me, leaning down closer to whisper into my ear. "All he wants is ah…the *inside scoop* on the Thompson story, just a little leverage to use for his press conference tonight."

"Sir, we're not politicians, we're news people."

"No, this is a business, one which happens to report the news. We have to survive and if possible make a profit. Look, it's gonna be public record tonight anyway. What's a few hours?"

"A lot if Manning is offering a huge payoff to our station," I reply.

"That's true, but when opportunity knocks …" He pats my back.

"… answer the door."

"Right, so what do you say? From what I hear, you have a hot little story. Why not make little change in process and boost your career?"

"Sir, I really need to get to Editing. Will you excuse me?"

"Miss Gomez, I really hate for you to pass up such an important opportunity."

"I'm sorry, Sir. My work is not for sale."

"Miss Gomez, people like you will never understand how this business truly works. I hate to see someone with such promise do something so stupid, but it's your career and your story. If you want to go down in flames with your so-called integrity, be my guest. You're free to go."

"Thank you, Sir," I say as I walk to Editing. Asshole. He was right though. Everybody in this business has an angle to play, but I refuse to help out that snake Manning. I don't care how many news copters he could buy. I'm not gonna be prostituted like a two dollar whore.

CHAPTER FOUR

BEDMATES
MR. DICKLIS

"Damnit! Stubborn Bitch!" I can't believe this little tramp is stonewalling this story. I would throw her out on her little ass if she weren't the best damn reporter in Indy.

As I walk back to my office I know I have to play it cool. I can't let my blood pressure get up, not today; too much riding on today. I open my office door; the sun is blinding my eyes through the back window. I feel knots tightening in my stomach when I see my cell phone walk across my desktop, vibrating like a junkie missing a fix. I stare at the thing, not wanting to answer it, for I know who it is and that it won't stop ringing. So I pick it up, sit down, and take a long breath.

"Hello?"

"What the fuck took you so long to answer the goddamn phone!"

"I'm sorry, Mr. Manning, I was talking to Theresa."

"Cool man! So what did you find out?"

"She won't budge."

"She won't budge! What you mean! You her boss, ain't ya?"

"Yeah but … ."

"Then make her ass tell you what the story is about!" Manning screams.

"She's a freelance reporter. If I bully her, she's likely to take herself to a rival station with her story."

"So this could be a hype up story for Thompson, a fluff piece, or for all we know it could be something about me and my side projects."

"I'm sure the focus on the story is Thompson."

"You sure about that? You wanna stake your word on that, Man?"

"No, Sir but…."

"Then you don't know shit! I have too much riding on this election to be surprised coming on up a couple weeks before the goddamn dance!"

"Sir, I will handle it. I promise you."

"You couldn't handle your dick in a fuckin' peepshow! Every piece of news about me, my opponents, or my business is approved by my camp before it hits the air! You know this! Every station in the city is down with this, and I expect you to keep on track. You know how much money I stand to lose if this election goes south?! I'm not losin' those contracts because you can't keep this ho' in check. You get that half-breed Nigga-Spic bitch on board with my program or its gonna get real ugly up in this motherfucker! Ya feel me, Bitch?"

"Ye … yes Sir," I manage to say.

"Class dismissed!" Manning hangs up the phone.

My heartbeat is pounding in my brain. Sweat pools on my face, my stomach burns, my hands start to shake. I need a fix. I loosen my tie. Two weeks … two weeks and this will all be over, the election will be settled and you can tell the devil to go screw himself. I reach in the drawer to get my heart medication and notice my .45. I pick it up and check the clip; it's fully loaded. I could just fire one between that black-hearted bastard's eyes.

"Mr. Dicklis?" There's a knock on the door, probably my secretary. "Mr. Dicklis?"

"Just a minute, Trina." I put my piece back and open the bottom drawer to grab my bottle of Vodka. I take a long, cool swig. What's this? I reach down and discover a little white pill. Vicodin. I need about forty of these but one and drink will do the trick. I take the pill and finish off the bottle. I get up and walk over to the mirror to check myself. It's like looking at a ghost in the cellar at midnight. Two more weeks and this shit will be over. Keep it together, old man. Keep it tight.

CHAPTER FIVE

CHILLY BALLS
KYLE

As Kyle and I walk to my truck, our eyes are set on the mission ahead. We wave at Michael heading home. I unlock the door and slide into the driver's seat, putting my backpack in the back seat.

Kyle slides into the passenger's side. "You and that damn bag," he says. "What are you, a terrorist or something? What's up with the bag man?"

"Nothing, man. You ready?"

Kyle clicks his seat belt. I start the ignition and back out of the parking lot en route to the Channel 10 Studio while Kyle leans back in the seat and interlocks his fingers, "So, man, how we gonna get this tape?"

"Shit if I know, Dude. I was about to ask you the same question."

"We could kidnap her."

"Yeah," I reply sarcastically.

54

"How about we cut the power to the building and sneak in and get the tape."

"Why don't we think of something that doesn't involve a felony conviction?"

"A'ight Dude, a'ight," Kyle says as he looks out at the window before closing his eyes.

Amidst the traffic gridlock, I notice two beautiful Sistas on their way to work. Their high heels and form-fitting business suits, a perfect complement to their coordinating briefcases, make the hard city streets come alive. I tap Kyle as I turn my head to take in another dose of their beauty.

"Damn, they fine! The darker the berry, the sweeter the juice!" Kyle says, damn near hopping out of the truck.

"You ain't lying. Damn it's been a long time since I got some."

"Dude, that's your fault, trying to play the saint role," he teases.

"Yeah, yeah, yeah," I roll my eyes, turning the steering wheel.

"You know that Theresa chick looks good as hell too. Maybe I should take out my trouser snake and put a spell on her. I've tamed many a mean coochie with Lil K here. Give me about four minutes, maybe seven. I'll have her ass speaking in dead languages!"

"Man, ain't nobody trying to see your knawled off dick. Come on, think of something realistic."

"Shit, I'm tryin,' Dude. Damn! I can't believe Mike got caught in some damn panties! Debra got his ass turned out! The shit we do for some pussy, man. Women don't even go through this much shit for the dick. I mean dick is like water in a faucet. All they have to do is turn the right knobs, and ta'dow, there it is. But us, we gotta navigate the Nile in a damn barrel to get the draws. And we keep doing this shit. I heard it's a man's world, but coochie rules the universe."

"I don't know, man. If you hit it just right that can tip the scales."

"What, you mean finding the elusive G-Spot? And what the hell does the 'G' stand for 'ghost,' cause I swear I'll find The Holy Grail before I find that shit and I be trying too, diggin' to the left, twistin' to the right, spinnin' on my head. I can't even enjoy sex cause I'm trying to make sure she get hers. Cause you know if you don't, she's gonna talk about your ass to her friends. Then her friend's friends gonna be talking about you until there's a damn

F.B.I., F.ucking B.eeyoch I.mpotent poster of your dumbass in the Post Office sayin 'Wanted: Kyle Limpy Thompson' for souring pussy all over town. Don't even bother. Just have Coke and a smile and cum on your own.' "

"You've given a lot of thought to this, haven't you?"

"Hell yeah, we gotta come correct. I had a girl get hers, roll over, belch, scratch her ass, fart, and go to sleep. I'm like 'what about me?'"

"You just a young buck, you need to slow down. Yeah, we still do more stupid shit to get the draws and yeah they have the power, but when you find a good one, you'll do that and a lot more for a woman's heart."

"I guess. Shit I ain't there yet. I'm still trying to get in as many pairs of panties as I can."

"A'ight, your prostate gonna pop. You just watch."

On the radio, a female announcer attracts my attention, "Hmmmm … Do you want harder, stronger, powerful, backbreaking sex?" Kyle turns the radio up. "You wanna make her scream your name in six different languages and have her begging for more? Do you want her to claw your back like a hungry tiger? Make your lover the envy of all her friends with The Rock power supplement. Made from all natural ingredients, including the authoritative power of Tygerknox, our special formula is derived from tiger testosterone. The Rock supplement will increase desire, potency, stamina, and size; yes size … ."

I turn the radio station, "I hate that shit, man. I can't believe people spend they money on that crap."

"You know what … between you and me, man, I tried it," Kyle confesses.

"You tried what?"

"The Rock."

"Bullshit."

"No, seriously."

"What? No!" I turn the radio off cause I know I'm not hearing this boy right.

"Yeah, man." Kyle smiles and looks out the window.

"I don't believe you. Did it work?" I ask, my curiosity getting the best of me.

"Man, I hit it so hard, I sent the chick to the hospital."

"What? Are you serious?"

"Yeah, Dude."

"Bull! Come on, man, give it up! When was this?"

"It was earlier this year, with Kelly, the three-hander."

"You kill me with that. So her ass is so big it takes three hands to cover it, huh?" I to had laugh, Kyle always came up with stupid shit like this.

"Yeah. It was nice little night to stay in, and get some trim. Kelly had a brownstone on the west side of town. She was staring out of the window watching the snow fall … "

I was playin' video games in Kelly's living room and hoping that her roommate wouldn't be coming home because Kelly was ready for some. She really looked sexy taking a sip of Merlot and running her hands up and the down her toned arms. A log in the fireplace crackled softly, warming the room as Kelly laid her head on the windowsill. Kelly's Coke-bottle shape looked real good against the soft fireplace light. She took another sip and brushed the wine glass across her cheek. Smiling, she slowly walked over to the couch like a tiger stalking prey. She stroked my face with the back of her hand, gently closed her eyes, and inhaled my cologne. She smirked and sat close to me on the couch, wrapping her arm around mine.

"It's beautiful outside. I just love the way the snowfall makes everything so pretty, like a soft, fleece blanket. I wish every night could be this way."

"I know it is beautiful out. I just hate driving in the mess," I said.

"Well ... it looks like we're snowed in and I would hate you to go outside in this weather. Carrie just called to tell me that she won't be home until late tomorrow night. On a cold night like tonight, I hate sleeping alone. A girl needs something warm to snuggle up to."

Pausing the game, I opened my legs and rested my arms on the back of the couch. Thinking she had got me, Kelly looked over at me and smiled. Who was I kiddin'? She was right; she did have me.

She reached back to gently pull out the bobby pins holding her brown ponytail up. "So, Mr. Thompson, since you have me trapped inside, whatever will we do?" She gently bit her bottom lip and pulled off her sweatshirt, showing a pair of massive breasts in a cream-colored bra. She took another sip of wine and straddled me on the couch.

When she slid my hands onto her ample backside, I shot up like a rocket. Our tongues made love, slipping into a deep kiss. I pulled her close and pressed her breasts firmly against my chest. My breath became shallow as I admired her large, dark, erect nipples yearning to be freed from the smooth bra pushing into my chest. Kelly moaned and swayed against my pelvis as my passion rose between her legs. I was so hard I could have burst right through her sweats. I leaned in and gently took her left breast and then the right into my mouth. My eyes lit up at the sight of her nipples peering through the wetness of the bra's velvet barrier, sending more hard pulses from my lap to her sweatpants.

She smiled, backed up, and rested her arms across my shoulders. "Since I see I have your full attention, can I ask you a question?"

"Wha' cha need, girl?" my voice gently vibrated.

"You think you can keep me warm and wet for the night?" A shiver went through my body. In that second, I was on fire. She pulled off my shirt and poured wine on my neck and chest. The soft warmth of her breath sent chills down my back as she kissed and licked the wine off my nipples. "Or am I on my own for the evening?"

"Well that might be a pretty big job, but I think I have just the tool for it." I reciprocated her seduction, deeply kissing her supple, wet lips.

Kelly placed my hands on her soft, large breasts. My mouth watered, squeezing them softly, wanting to rub her long, stiff nipples all over my face and chest. She leaned into my ear, "I hope you know how to work a nine iron, 'cause I definitely need to take more than just a *couple* of strokes off my game."

My heart skipped a beat; I had to have her. I picked her up and carried her to the bedroom to lay her on the bed.

"I'll be right back, girl."

She grabbed my shoulders and pulled me down on to the bed, "Don't make me wait too long." We shared another kiss. She had me so twisted, my knees started to buckle as I crashed into the doorframe to leave the room. I guess Kelly thought that was funny, for she giggled as she walked over to her dresser. I eventually made it to the living room and opened my backpack. I wiped the sweat off my forehead and reached into my backpack taking out a medicine bottle.

"The Rock Sexual Enhancer. Take one per six hours, for longer, stronger, more powerful sex." I smirked, tracing my fingers over my mustache as I

stared at Kelly in the other room, rubbing cocoa
butter on her long runner's legs. I took a deep breath,
trying to savor the moment and popped a pill. She
stripped down to her panties and sprayed perfume on
her heaving cocoa colored full tits. She took off the
bra and ran her fingers through her hair. Damn she
looked good. I was frozen stiff all over watching this
ebony goddess in the distance.

"Damn she fine," I whispered, taking another
pill as I grabbed a condom and walked toward the
bedroom. Kelly met me in the hallway and took off
my clothes. Our bodies intertwined as we slipped into
the bedroom. I slipped on the rubber, and ecstasy
flowed through me as we enjoy our winter night's
passion. She smiled drawing my manhood deep
inside her wet, sumptuous walls. I've always loved it
when woman smiled during sex.

In the truck, I pat the sweat from my brow as
I listened to Kyle's story, "Damn, it sounds like ya'll
could have turned the heat off in the crib, man."

"Oh yeah Bro, it was the bomb. I wish I
could have sent some your way. I'm beatin' it up like
a circus monkey and, Dude, it was good. Oh shit, it
was good, damn near platinum! Damn man, she's got

some skills. So she says, 'Let me back into that big dick, boy.' So I just had to comply."

"It's a tough job, but I'm sure you were the Brotha to handle it, huh?"

Kyle scraped his bottom lip against his front teeth, "For sho, Dude, for sho! So we switched to doggie style. I dragged her to the foot of the bed, put on my boots, and dug in deep. You know I gotta hear the ass clap against my stomach. I'm doing the Jackhammer Teabag, and we're in the spot. You know that moment where you and your girl are so into that you don't care the bedroom could be on fire, and you say fuck it, I'm cumming. We were in the zone … ."

I reached behind me and slid my hand across the dresser knocking over Kelly's perfumes and lotions onto the floor.

"Hey … Boy wait a minute. What you doing?" She asked looking back at the mess.

"Don't worry about it, Gal." I said as I wrapped my arms around her and lifted her onto the dresser. I raised up on my toes and reunited with her. She wrapped her arms and legs as tightly around me as she could. Her lips covered every inch of my neck

I dug my toes in the carpet, thrusting into her and lifting off the dresser top. The top piece of the dresser slides forward. She reached back to hold it up. Our bodies harmonized in perfect sync to achieve the nirvana our bodies need more than food, water, even air. I pushed as far as I could, curling her toes hard. Her mouth opened wide, yet she can't scream; passion claimed her voice. The fire between us rose higher … higher … and higher until we melted into one. We climaxed into each other and collapsed to the bed out of breath.

I gripped the steering wheel, "Damn you must have been tearing it up. She got a sister?"

"Naw, man this is one of a kind. I tell you The Rock was bomb because as soon as I started to cum my dick swelled up."

"Really?"

"Oh yeah, man, it got fat. I guess it makes sense,'cause some animals' dicks get bigger when they cum."

"I'm scared to even ask how you know some shit like that."

"Well, man I'm telling you it worked 'cause my shit got huge."

"So tell me how this can possibly go south?"

"We both climaxed and collapsed in a spooning position on the bed … "

Kelly hummed and rubbed her hands across her chest. Man she had some nice ones. Every muscle in my body was exhausted but elated.

"That was so good, Baby. You were an animal. What got into you?"

"I guess we just fit so well together." I nibbled on Kelly's right earlobe. "Why don't you do me a favor and drop it like it's hot so I can get recharged."

"Hmmm, you think Lil' K can *rise* to the occasion again?"

"Like my granddaddy used to say, I can show better than I can tell you. Shake that ass!" I said smacking her butt.

"Yes, Sir!" Kelly saluted and dropped to all fours giving me a show. I looked over to the floor to see a tube a KY Jelly. Kelly laid on her back and sent fireworks off inside me at the sight of her placing one of her massive breasts in her mouth.

"DAMN!!!!" I said biting my fist as I squatted down to pick up the KY. My eyes were stuck on her lips around her half dollar sized nipple, bring me back to full mass.

"Oh yeah, Baby, I gotta tap dat ass."

"Well, if you feeling froggie, jump, Boy. Hit this ass from the back." Kelly turned over, laid her head down on a pillow, and arched her back. I sucked in some air through my teeth and felt around behind me for the tube. I picked it up and immediately squirted Kelly's butt, slipped off the condom, grabbed my dick and my balls, and started smackin' her with it like a belt. Swacky, swack, one. Swacky, swack, two. Swacky, swack, three. Then it happened.

"What?" I ask rolling the window down, eagerly anticipating the rest of the story.

"Well, here's where the story goes south."

I smacked Kelly on the butt for the third time, but this time I couldn't move my dick off of her. I looked down at Lil K, stuck to Kelly's butt cheek like welded steel.

"Damn Baby, you got the KY heating liquid, didn't you?" I asked her. " It's feeling kinda hot, I can't wait to feel this in Ms. Kitty. Come on, give me another taste."

I violently tried to jerk myself off of Kelly, but Lil K was not budging. Now, I was getting nervous. "

"Baby, come on. What are you doing? Come on, don't keep me waiting, Boy. I'm about to give you a coochie line of credit with Platinum benefits."

"Uh … uh … I think I need a minute."

"A'ight I want some juice anyway. I'll be back." Kelly pulled forward, and I moved with her.

Kelly smiled. "Damn, Baby I know you like it, but don't worry, I'll be back."

Kelly pulled forward again, but I'm still stuck to her. Kelly jerked harder, jerking me harder behind her.

"Come on now, Kyle. I'm thirsty."

Kelly yanked again and again, pulling me all over the bed with her.

"Stop playin,' Kyle. Come on."

"Baby … uh … um … I don't know how to tell you this, but I think we're stuck together."

"Yeah, right."

I jerked back. This had to be a dream. I pressed my hands against her back and tried to push away, "I ain't playin … I … I can't get off of you."

"What are you talking about? This is ain't funny no more. I gotta pee."

Kelly yanks away as hard as she can only to have me slam into the back of her.
"What the fuck, Kyle!!! Come on!"

"I'm telling you I'm not playin' I think we're stuck."

"Stuck?! What the hell you mean, stuck? How?! That's impossible."

"I don't know, but it ain't moving."

I reached over to the floor and picked up the tube I squirted Kelly with, "I don't know. All I did was put this … K-Y Jelly you had and … oh shit! Oh Shit! SHIT!" My lips shook. I put my index finger in my mouth and gently bit it trying to figure out how I was gonna tell this girl this little bit of information.

"What … what?"

"Oh, fuck me!"

"What, goddamnit, what?"

"Umm … uh … .ummm."

"Um … uh. … what, Boy?!"

"This!"

I handed Kelly the tube. I thought her eyes were gonna pop out. She put her hand over her mouth to catch the scream inside. Her mood switched from passion to pissed in a flash.

"AW Hell No, Kyle! You have got to be fuckin kidding me! You didn't!!"

"I'm sorry! I'm sorry!!"

"How the fuck did you grab my Standax Welder's Adhesive? I use this shit to weld construction grade plastics at work! You know what this is? This shit is basically extra, extra, strength super glue! Oh, fuck me!"

I looked back and noticed Kelly's toolbox was knocked over on the floor along with her perfumes and lotions. Kelly jerked forward hard. I followed, smacking into the back of her and knocking her off the bed. When she got up and the tried to run to the bathroom, she slammed me into the wall.

Kelly reached back, pushing the palm of her hand into my chest. She tried to push me off of her, but I wouldn't budge, "What are we gonna do! Shit, I can't believe this! How bad is it?"

"The … the … head and almost all the shaft is stuck, plus some hair…and one ball."

"And one ball." She mocked me sarcastically. She pissed me off sayin' that shit, but I couldn't be too mad. I'd be pissed too with a throbbing dick stuck in the crack of my ass.

My eyes lit up, "The shower, maybe some soap and hot water!"

"This shit is waterproof!" she said with a cracked voice.

"Well we gotta try."

"Aaargh, fine!"

We waddled over to the shower and desperately tried to wash the glue out.

"Can you move it? Can you? Can you?" Kelly asked hysterically.

"No, it's jammed on there tight."

"Fuck, Kyle!" She said slamming her fist into the shower wall knocking down a tile.

"Calm down. We'll figure something out."

Kelly spun her head around and with a stupid, surprised look said, "We'll figure something out?! Arrgh!" Suddenly her eyes moved to the left and then to the right. She frowned and asked in a loving, sarcastic voice, "Kyle, baby why are you still hard?"

"Uh, it must be the supplement."

"What supplement, Love?" Kelly asked in the same sarcastic voice.

"Well I sort of took a sexual enhancer, that one off the radio."

"What, The Rock? Are you serious? Are you flippin' serious?"

"Yeah, I wanted to give you a little extra ummmph tonight."

"A little extra ummmph? Oh this shit *can't* be happening!"

"I'm sorry, Baby. I'm sorry. I'm so sorry!"

"Just shut your sorry ass up! What we gonna do?! What we gonna do?! Okay, maybe if you lose your erection you can peel it off real quick, like a waxing. All right make it go down."

"I can't just turn it off," I explained.

"Well, think of something … something unsexy."

I closed my eyes hard and grunted, "It ain't working, all I see is ass."

"We gotta do something! Damnit, I can't believe this shit! Ice! We'll try some ice!" We waddled to the kitchen. Kelly opened the freezer and gave me an ice cube. I grabbed it and cringed, rubbing it on my dick as we baby stepped back to the bathroom.

"Is it going down?" she asked hopefully.

"No, now all I have an icy, hard dick."

"This shit ain't funny, Boy!"

"I can't believe I'm about to say this. Okay, hit me in my free ball. That should work. Then maybe I can snatch it off real quick."

She seemed all too happy to do that shit. She quickly grabbed a shower back brush.

I braced myself, "Okay. On three. One … "

72

This bitch immediately reaches between her legs and slams the brush into my crouch.

I grunted, slumped over, slipped on the bathroom floor, and fell through the shower curtains, tearing them off, as we hit the floor, still stuck together.

I began crying and wheezing, "Aw, damn, you bent it!"

"Are you're still hard?" Kelly asked looking over her shoulder.

"Yeah, damn."

"What we gonna do? Shit!"

"All right, call 911."

Kelly quickly lifted up off her shoulder and asked, "Are you high? You know my parents are EMT's. I am not about to risk my father coming here. Figure something else out!"

"Well, you gonna have to bite the bullet and call for help."

"My father got pissed at me when I got my hand caught in his favorite cookie jar and we had to break it to get my hand out. I am not about to call him and tell that man I got a dick stuck on my ass!"

"Well, what we gonna do? I know. I'll call my boy Darryl."

"Darryl, the back alley, bootleg mechanic? What the fuck is he supposed to do?"

"Well he's a locksmith too."

"A fuckin locksmith? I don't need a Nigga with a crowbar right now! We ain't fuckin' breakin' into crates, I need somebody with more than a damn sixth grade education!"

"Then what do you suggest, Dear? Wait ain't … um … um … your girl Tina. She's studying to be a nurse. Shit, call her."

"No damnit, I always make fun of her because she, goes down on every Dude on the second date. I always call her a freaky bitch. If I call her, I'll never hear the end of this shit. She'll come here, with a fuckin' film crew in tow!"

"You guys use this stuff at work. Somebody there has got to have gotten stuck. Maybe they can help or there's a hot line or something."

"Yeah let me just call 'the dick stuck on my ass hotline!' Pass me the motherfuckin' phone! We use gloves so this type of shit don't happen."

"Well, shit girl, you gonna have to bend if we want to get out of this."

"Come on, let's go to the kitchen."

We got back to the kitchen and tried everything, bacon grease, butter, lemon juice, fatback, baby oil, but nothing worked.

"All right come on. Help me get my clothes on. We'll go to Arnett Hospital across town."

So the sun was coming out, she put on a skirt, I put my jeans on, and we went to the garage to go to the hospital. We shuffled to Kelly's car, a two-door hatchback. Kelly took out the keys and unlocked the door as I stopped staring at the car.

"Kelly, how we gonna get to the hospital?"

"What do you mean? We'll drive. Come on."

"Drive in what, this shiny dickhead on wheels?"

"So, it's a little tight."

"So ... explain to me how we gonna fit in the driver's seat, draw me the diagram of how this shit is gonna work."

"Just sit down and put my legs up like this."

We wiggled in the car, trying to figure out how to fit in together. We must have tried a dozen positions to make it work; Kelly on top, me on the side, Kelly hanging out the side of the car with the door open; nothing worked. We end up in a spooning position, on our sides, half way out the car.

"I can't reach the pedals", I groaned.

"Well hook your leg over the steering wheel."

I strained, trying to twist into a position to drive.

"This ain't gonna work, shit! We gotta do something. This is a nightmare, and are you still hard?!"

"I can't help it!"

She mocked me again. "'I can't help it.' I can't believe you did this shit!"

"Me! 'I'm a nasty girl watch this ass! Make me cum!'"

"What kind of dumbass puts superglue on his dick in the first place?"

"You had it by the bed!"

"It wasn't by the bed, it was in a toolbox that your ass dumbass knocked over. How the fuck you mistake a tube of Standax for KY Jelly?"

"Fuck, I was in the moment!"

"Fuck, you was in the moment?! I swear, Kyle. You have the fuckin' intelligence of plant life! I swear to God if I look dumbass up in the dictionary, I'd find a picture of your ass between da, doofus, dullard, dumb, dummy, and doh!"

"Man, fuck you Kelly."

"I swear, my little bother is intelligent enough to not get himself in this kind of shit."

"Your brother is eleven. Why would he even have his dick on your ass?"

"Oh, I swear you a stupid motherfucker."

"Fuck you!"

"That's the problem, you men always think with the wrong head, the smaller of the two at that! Your brain is lodged in the crack of my ass, and I gotta do the thinking for both of us. And you're still hard?"

"I … can … not … help … it! It's … The … Rock!"

"Rock my ass!"

"I did, that's how we got in the shit now!"

"You conceited Bastard!"

Kelly struggled to get free, rocking the car back and forth, "Fuck!"

An hour passed, and she started crying. I wrapped my arms around her. We closed our eyes and begin to accept our fate. I grabbed her hand tenderly.

"Look, I'm sorry we got into this."

"Kyle, I know you didn't mean for this to happen. Maybe this is a sign. I gotta change my life, that I gotta make a change." Kelly sank into me, looking for some warmth, probably to blanket her shame.

"Don't be hard on yourself. This could happen to anyone."

"Oh, yeah, this shit happened to me just last week."

"That's not what I meant. Anyway, come on. Let's get out of the car and stretch out."

We slid out of the car, and Kelly wiped the tears from her face, "I guess I'll call 91 ... Wait!! Wait. I got an idea! I can't believe I didn't think of this before!"

Kelly dragged me to a corner of the garage. She yanked back a sheet with my Harley underneath it.

"I can't believe that I forgot your bike was here. Come on we're getting out of here." Kelly said gliding her hand across the bike's seat.

"Kelly, it's like four, five feet of snow on the ground!"

She got mad, "I don't care! You get your ass on that bike, and get my ass to the hospital; and get your dick off of it. NOW!"

At this point, I'd try anything. We figured our way onto the bike with Kelly putting her legs over the handlebars. My hands barely reached the bars as I started the ignition. Kelly opened the garage door. I reved the engine and gunned it out the garage. The bike flew over the snow bank in front of the garage door. We leaned back on the bike, slipping and sliding down the street.

Kelly held down her skirt, "How you doing back there?"

"Jack Frost is nippin' at my nuts." I said spitting out Kelly's hair blowing in my mouth.

"I think we're about ten miles from hospital."

Five minutes later, a Siren blared and red and blue lights flashed behind us. "Oh shit, I thought as my heart pounded violently at the thought of what we were going to tell this cop.

I looked behind me, "Oh shit! I'm only goin' 15 MPH."

"I think the fact that my coochie is coolin' in the wind, may have something to do with our friend back there. Shit, he ain't passing us. You better pull over."

The officer pulled off the side of the road behind us. He looked over me leaning back and Kelly holding down her skirt.

"Nice morning for a ride, huh?" he asked. "I was just thinking about taking my bike out too. Only one problem, there's four feet of snow on the ground! So which one of you bikers want to start talking?"

"Officer Sir, you are not gonna believe the night we have had," I said wiping my face. "Have you ever heard of The Rock supplement?"

"Yeah, that sex pill on the radio?"

"Well, you see what had happened was…"

We shared our story with the cop. He didn't even care that its only ten degrees outside as he listens stone-faced to us. He put his hands on his hips and chewed on the toothpick dangling from his mouth.

"Let me get this straight, you put superglue on your penis?"

"Yes, Sir."

"And, ma'am, you let this genius put his penis, covered in superglue, on your butt?"

"Ah, yes Sir."

"And, to boot, you took a dose of a sexual supplement, and now you can't get it down or off of her. Plus your cheeks are stuck together?"

"Yes, Sir," we both answer. I just knew I was going to the booty house then.

"And now, you both are on the way to the hospital to pry your cheeks apart and pull your penis off her butt?"

"Yes, Sir," we replied.

"Get off the bike. I need to do a sobriety test."

The cop looked us over. The wind must have picked up as Kelly held down her skirt. The officer looked between us. "Damn, boy, you might be telling the truth. How the fu … and girl how did you let this … I need back up. Wait, right there."

The cop stepped away from us and grabbed his radio, "47 to base. 47 to base."

"Go ahead", a voice answered on the radio.

"I need a supervisor, a female officer, a … a … fire truck and … a uh … ambulance and ... You know what? Just bring one of everything to the 3700 block of Meridian."

"This is Sergeant Hunter. What's going on, Officer Black?"

"Sir, honestly I can't … even explain … over the radio. You gotta see this."

"What is going on, Officer Black!"

"Sir, I need you to 10-41 to 5. 10-41 to 5."

"10-4 switching to 5."

Officer Black handed us a blanket and switched his radio to channel 5 and proceeded to tell his sergeant about us. Minutes passed. Kelly listened to radio, the cold wind didn't phase her. I guess it couldn't compare to the chill of her parents' embarrassment if her secret got out. When Officer Black turned his back to us, Kelly turned her head to me and asked, "What do you think they're gonna do to us?"

"Maybe they'll give us a break."

Suddenly laugher exploded on the radio, followed by, "I can't believe this! This is too good to be true. I gotta see this and am en route with assistance."

"10 … 10 … oh shit … 10-4, Sir." Officer Black closed his eyes tight, trying to compose himself as he turned to us. Our heads were down.

He snickered, "Don't worry. I'm sorry." Officer Black put his head down on his police cruiser. His body jerked violently as he laughed with his head in his arms. A half minute later he rose and wiped the tears from his face. "Okay, help is on the way. Oh God, I'm sorry, man. If I was her, I'd be whuppin' your ass. I'd be unglued!" Officer Black slapped his hand over his mouth, "Oh I'm sorry. That was kinda hard, wasn't it? Look, here comes help."

The emergency crews made their way to us. Everyone snorted, trying to hold the laughter in. Kelly looked out of the window as we headed to the hospital. She covered her face as the crews hit the ground laughing.

The police officer driving looked back at us and said, "Don't worry, we are almost to the hospital. I would have gotten their sooner but we were … were … all jammed up."

I grip the steering wheel of the truck hard listening to Kyle's story, "Oh my god, Dude. You have got to be joking. There is no way. I would have given a paycheck to have seen that shit."

"It's true. I got the dick marks to prove it. You don't believe me? You wanna see." He starts to unzip his pants.

"Naw, man, naw. I guess you the only Negro to have a piece of ass with you all the time."

"Yeah I know," Kyle grimaces.

I hold my cramped stomach, exhaled deeply, and wiped my red eyes. "So what happened at the hospital?"

"After the nursing crew and doctor laughed their asses off, they separated us. Kelly and I ain't spoke since."

"Damn, I wouldn't speak to your goofy ass either, but a'ight, Dude, a'ight. Back to business. The tape."

"Yeah, man, I don't know. We'll probably just have to...damn, Bro, check this out! Damn she fine! Kinda tomboyish but still. X, you seeing this shit?" Kyle shouts at me.

"Here you go." I glance over seeing a woman pull up beside us on a bad ass BMV motorcycle next to the truck at a stoplight.

"Damn, she's fine! I gotta holla at her. Pull this shit over, man."

"Let me see what you looking at.", I roll down the window and I lean over to focus in on this biker beauty. I look over her sculpted body, packed into a tight yellow body suit. She brushes back her long brown hair from her face and looks up at the truck.

My heart sinks, "Oh, hell, no! Oh you gotta be fuckin' kiddin' me!"

CHAPTER SIX

THE BOOTY GODS
JESSE & XAVIER

The Biker takes off her shades, smiles, and says, "Hey, Xavier, how you doing, baby?"

Of all the people to see on a day like today, I can't believe this trollop is here smiling in my face. If there weren't a fuckin' car in front of me, I would run this light.

"I'm fine, Sonja," I say, frowning from the truck.

"You sure are, Boy." Sonja says, slightly unzipping her motorcycle jacket as she speaks. She's already got Kyle's nose wide open. He's drooling over himself at the sight of her cleavage. I roll my eyes, focusing on the stoplight wishing it would change.

"Damn, she got some biggins in that jacket," Kyle whispers to me. "She'd make a homeboy wanna be a better man."

Sonja revs her bike and asks, "How's J. doing? Why don't you tell him hi for me, baby."

I'm still staring at the stoplight, "Man, fuck you, Sonja."

"Aw, don't be that way X Baby. Why don't you give me a call, and we can go out sometime? Is this cutie your lil' brother?"

"Take yo ass on, Sonja!"

Sonja blows me a kiss, pops a wheelie, and speeds away. I turn onto another street, then another, and another, trying to put as much distance between her and us as I can before I run her over with my truck.

Kyle twists around, "Did you see the ass on that? I love biker chicks!"

"Crazy ass bitch," I mumble.

"Damn, you don't normally talk about the females like that. Why you don't like her? What, you hit that?"

"Hell naw! Hell no!"

"Then what's going on with her?"

"My boy Jesse used to go out with her."

"Goofy-ass, numb nut Jesse hit that?! Come on! Man, he makes Urkel look like Jay-Z. Quit playin'."

"Man, I'm tellin' you the God's honest truth. Jesse wasn't always like that. He used to be the coolest kat that the kitties loved to put that tail up to. I remember last year. Dude just came out of law school, got this phat job downtown, nice ride, a big house on the north side of town. I went to check his new place out a year ago ... "

I read the sign in front of the luxury upscale community that said "Dash Oaks". I've been by this neighborhood dozens of times, but I've never known anyone who actually lived there. Living in Dash Oaks means you made it, not only that, but you were it. It was cool to see one of us there, living the good life. I was amazed at the large homes, standing like monuments of success. I came to the end the neighborhood, where I pulled into the driveway of a large house on a hill.

"Damn, this crib is plush," I thought to myself as I grabbed my overnight bag and made my way to the huge front door, which seemed to vibrate as I rang the doorbell to the massive house.

Jesse opened the door. "What up, dawg! What up! Come in, man!"

"Playa, playa!"

We hugged as I looked around the living room. "Damn Dude, you livin' large out here with the white folks."

"Yeah, good year and even better realtor. You'd be surprised, what the right investment portfolio and a thick dick will get you."

"Thick dick? What'd you do screw the realtor?"

"And her mama."

"And her mama? Aw man, you ain't changed a bit since college, ever the ho," I said.

"Dude, if the getting is good, I'm gonna get it. You still playing the saint roll, huh?"

"Nah, I'm just chillin,'" I replied.

"Let your nuts keep chillin', they gonna drop off."

I came across a picture on an end table, "Who is this little dip?"

Jesse took the photo, "Ah, man, that's Sonja. This little honey and I hooked up on the west side. I met her ten months ago when the firm contracted her to do some electrical work on the building, and man I gotta say, the booty is sweet. You know I like 'em thick, man. She's just one of the many flavors in the candy shop."

"Damn, I like her. I'd be getting in that right now if I were you,".

"I'm just letting it stay at home and marinate," Jesse explained. "She's kinda getting possessive, call herself wanting to have a little attitude man, but I got that ass on lock down."

"What, she trying to rope you with the c-word?"

"Commit? Yeah, man, she pulling the old pussy card, saying I can't hit it unless I stay with it. I tell her we're just friends with benefits. I try to keep it real."

"And I bet she keep the draws up REAL tight after that shit too?"

"Naw, man that's the thing, she still let me hit it too. Like the other night, she comes over at 2 in the morning … "

It was raining real hard outside and the doorbell was ringing for like twenty minutes. I thought I was hearing things as I walked to the front door rubbing the sleep out my eyes. I opened the door to see Sonja, standing in a yellow skintight body suit.

"Hola, baby. What's up? Can I come in?"

"Girl," I looked at my watch. "It's two in the morning. You couldn't call?"

"I just couldn't sleep. You know thunder and lighting scares me, I just needed a big, strong pair of arms around me."

Sonja stepped in and wrapped her arms around my shoulders. She pressed her soft, wet lips across mine. As much as I wanted to sleep, I woke up at that point, for there is nothing like waking up to a piece of ass. I slipped into the pleasure of her touch, letting my hands explore the curves of her soft brown body. She put my hands on her butt and squeezed her hands over mine. Her ass was soft as Jello; it was like I was making dough for pizza. I moaned, letting her know I was awake. She could already tell if there was any feeling between her legs cause my johnson was thumping the shit out of her thighs. I pulled her closer. She smiled as she started to make a path down my chest with her lips, "Wouldn't you like it to always be this way?"

"Damn." I pulled away slightly, "Here you go."

Sonja stepped closer pressing her tits against my chest. "It's just that we've been dating a long time, baby. We obviously care for one another. Our bodies obviously like each other...." Sonja turned around and pressed her butt into my dick, rubbing her cheeks against my shaft. Her damn outfit was so tight it was like she had another layer of skin. I swear I could feel the lace in her panties on my dick. She placed my hands on her titties and leaned back to rub her lips against mine. Her long brown hair was like silk, just like her pussy. "Why don't we take this to another level?" she asked seductively.

"Girl, damn I like you, but I don't...."

Sonja placed her index finger on my lips, "Shhhh...don't say a thing, just sit down. Let me give you a taste of how I treat my man."

Sonja reached in her purse and took out a CD. She put it in the stereo and dimmed the lights. She walked over to the bar and poured me a drink. I sat down on the couch, ready to see what this girl had in store for me. Sade's "Is it a Crime?" played on the stereo. Sonja handed me a scotch glass and began to dance. I took a sip of Brandy as I watched Sonya slowly remove her clothes, piece by piece. My heart fluttered, my stomach dropped as she rubbed her hands all over her body. Sade's voice filled the house, flowing around Sonja and complementing her movements perfectly.

Shit, this was making me hot. I knew I wasn't going back to sleep without a taste of her that night. I watched, licking my lips under beads of sweat forming on my forehead. I gripped the glass, wanting to wait and savor the experience. I took another sip to calm the fire growing inside. Sonja's movements were like wax gliding down a hot candle on a sultry summer's night. I rubbed my thighs, trying to fight the urge to throw her on the ground and take her right then and there. Five minutes passed, and I wiped the glass clean, placing it against my forehead. Sonja looked down at the empty glass covered in steam. She knew she had me in the palm of her hand. I was feelin' faded, and it was time to get X-rated.

She smiled and slinked over to me. Her perfect naked body overloaded every nerve in my body. I couldn't stand this teasing anymore. I threw her on the couch and fucked the shit out of her.

An hour later I had her bent. I lit a Cuban and smiled, looking over Sonja knocked out on the couch. I grabbed her body suit, wiped off the jeez on my thigh and the floor, went to my bedroom, and shut the door and was out for the night.

The next afternoon, I finally woke up. I was feeling funny but refreshed. Pussy always made me feel like a new man. I rubbed my head and shook off the disorientation of a long night's sleep. I walked in the living room and saw that Sonja left a little panty souvenir in the middle of the floor. I picked up the red thongs and took a sniff. "Ah, Sonja … ."

I rubbed my chin, grinning at Jesse's reminiscent tale. "Sounds sweet, man. Why don't you want to commit? Ya'll seem to get along, she sounds like she takes care of you. Shit, I wish I could find someone like that."

"She's great! She gives me everything I want or need. She cooks like Emeril, cleans like a surgeon, and screws like a million dollar ho."

"So, what's the problem?"

"Technically, I told her she was my only girlfriend. So we kinda have a boyfriend and girlfriend thang going on, but shit I'm getting too much pussy right now! I'm getting White pussy, Black pussy, Asian pussy, Spanish pussy, Eskimo pussy, I'm getting it from all sides. I'm pussy globetrotting right now. The Booty Gods only bestow you with X amount of chances to hit it. When the time comes, you have to seize the opportunity. Carpe the draws! Slay all beasts. Come on, stop acting like you a saint. I'm your boy, and I know you've been through your list of panties too."

"True, true, but I'm telling you a dime may show up everyday, but a gold piece don't. There's a lot of chicken heads out there, especially since you're coming up."

"You ain't understanding, Man. I'm a hustler. I don't play the game, I change it. This is my world Man. Why you do you think I got the pussy palace here? To get more pussy! You need to take advantage, Dude. These bitches know what's up. They act like the victims, but they playas too. We have to go out and work ten to twelve hour shifts so we can buy the nice cars to pick them up and drive them to the nice houses for them, and all they have to do is lay on their back and take this fat dick. And then they want to complain about that half the time? You tell me, who playin' who? I'm just leveling the playing field, man."

I looked Jesse up and down with slight disgust. This Dude has just gotten beside himself. "A'ight man, so when am I gonna get to meet this chick? Tell her to bring over some friends."

"She call herself mad at me right now. Earlier this week, she calls on the phone at 12:30 in da morning and asked to come over. In fact, it was one of the rare times she called before coming over, which was good because I had a little somethin', somethin' on the deck … "

It was a quiet warm, dry, summer night out. Well, it was quiet except for Melissa, my secretary and new Scandinavian conquest, screaming her damn head off on my deck. I'm surprised nobody called the cops. I was tapping dat ass from behind, grabbing a handful of Melissa's long blond hair, pulling her pale muscle toned body close to me. Frankly she was lovin' this shit, crying out like I got the biggest dick she ever had. Probably was. Shit, I thought she was gonna choke to death on it when she went down on me. Anyway, my cell phone rings, we ignore it and continue fuckin'. The phone stops ringing and a minute it later started again. I was getting pissed, so I tried to look at the phone on the chair. I was squinting to focus in on the number, without pulling out of Melissa. The phone stopped ringing and starts again ten minutes later.

I reached down to get it. "Oh, damn Melissa, I swear your shit is like butter. A brotha could get used to this. Shit, you feel good! Damn who is this on the fuckin' phone, probably the goddamn office." I knew exactly who it was, shit she was getting on my nerves. I had looked at the caller ID and saw Sonja's number.

Melissa continued panting and moaning. "Aw ... yeah ... yeah ... shit, baby don't get it."

"Naw, I gotta take this. I'll hurry up, you just keep backing that sexy ass up and be quiet ... "

I answered the cell, "Ye ... yeah ... Hel ... Hello."

"Hey Baby what's up? What you doing?"

"Nothing, ah ... just working out. How are things on your end?"

"Had a long day. Worked a lot of contracts today. Boy, I missed you today. Can I come over? I wanna see you."

"Well, I'm heading out in a minute. I have some briefs to wrap up. I can handle that issue a little later if you like."

"Handle that issue?"

"I'm sorry, I just got a lot on my plate now. Let … let me call you back."

"Everything okay, baby?"

"Ye ... yeah I'm just working on some thangs."

"Okay then, I love you, Boo."

"That's nice, same here. Take care." I hung up the phone and continued to hammer fuck Melissa.

I leaned against the countertop, "So did you ever hook up with Sonja?"

"Naw, I had to get another taste of that sweet vanilla, gushy stuff. Tore the pussy in half! Ha, Ha. Fucked her from the bedroom to right there on that countertop. I wiped the floor with that ass."

I subtlety backed away from the countertop. "Did you at least stop by her place?"

"Naw man, I didn't have the chance to. The Booty Gods … "

"… let me guess, have rained many a blessing upon you."

"Yep, since we hooked up last night I figured every thing was cool. But I see where you're going, I'll send her a couple of dozen roses at her shop and take her out. A little wine, chocolate, and a big johnson always do the trick. Come on, I want you to check out my new toy."

We walked down to the family room. I sat down on the couch as Jesse opened the television cabinet to reveal a nice ass sixty-inch TV. "I just got this last week. State of the art, High Definition, Surround sound. Check this out. It's even got a fridge in the lower compartment."

"Aw man, that's tight! What's this, oak?"

"Hell, yeah, Dude. I gotta do big in the pussy palace!" Jesse looked through DVD cabinet. "What you wanna watch? Did you see *Kill Bill*?"

"Hell, yeah, but we can check that out again man. Anything with Tarantino is the shit. He could make Goldilocks and The Three Little Bears and it would be some wicked shit. Goldilocks would be shooting up in the forest. The baby bear would a hitman. The papa bear would be a pimp ho'in out the seven dwarfs."

"Yeah, 'ol boy has got some mad film skills."

Jesse passed me a beer, and I sank into the black Corinthian leather couch as the movie started.

"Lucy Lui is the bomb, Man. She's just perfect. I'm mean just fucking perfect," I casually commented.

"So you'd like to hit that, huh? You like a little chop suey action?" Jesse asked me.

"I don't know if it is just the roles that she plays or if it is just her, man, but that girl is beautiful. I don't think I could hit it. I'd just be staring at her."

"Man you soundin' kinda whipped, Dude. When's the last time you got some?"

"Don't worry about that, I'm a'ight."

"Uh-huh, Lucy Lui's all right, I like Vivca myself. That girl is sexy! Q.T. did her wrong in this movie though. Oh man, you gotta check this out. Let me kick on the surround sound."

Jesse grabbed the remote. The volume gets louder at first then seconds later a high-pitched squeal comes from the T.V. like an airplane engine revving up for take off. A second later the T.V. screen blows up. We sat on the couch, dumbfounded, as sparks fall from the screen. Jesse was still holding the remote in the same position pointed to the T.V. My mouth was just stuck open. A minute later the T.V. falls face first onto the floor.

Jesse leaped up and stares at the remote, "What the fuck? I just bought this shit! Fuck! Fuck! FUCK! FUCK!"

"Damn…" was all I could say.

"What the hell!"

"Good thing it is still under warranty, huh?" I said lamely. My words offered no comfort to Jesse.

"Fuck! I guess man. Let me unplug it. Shit!"

Jesse got up and walked toward the television, suddenly the DVD drawer flung open, shooting the disc out across the room. It shot out so fast that it lodged into the couch where Jesse's head would be if he were sitting down. We both stared at the wall as the DVD drawer slowly closed back. This is some freaky shit.

I got up and stumbled away from the couch. "Maybe the T.V. doesn't like Tarantino."

Jesse threw the remote against the wall, "Man, this is some bullshit! I'm telling you I'm taking this back to store and getting two T.V.s! I may even sue their asses for mental distress. I can't believe this! Fuck!"

Jesse took a breath and flopped down on the couch, "I'm sorry, Dude. I'm cool, I'm cool. Come on. I got another T.V. down the hall. I can't believe this crap. Five thousand motherfuckin' dollars I paid for that piece of crap!"

We walked through the house to the other room. Suddenly, the chandler in the dining room cashed into the glass table below.

I hit the dirt. "Damn!" I exclaimed.

"Aw DAMN! My mama gave me this table! What's next?" Jessie moaned as we looked up at the ceiling.

"Man, it looks like you might have a termite or rodent problem or something," I suggested.

"Man, I believe it. Since we're near the lake, there's all types of bugs and shit around here. The exterminator is coming out on Monday."

"That is the only thing about living near the water, that and the flooding."

"Don't remind me, but this place is a pussy magnet."

"You kill me, Jesse. We up the are asses in glass and you still thinking about the draws."

"Got to keep the eyes on the prize Dude. Cause the Booty Gods only … "

"… bestow so many blessings upon a brotha. I know, I know. I'll help you clean up this shit."

We cleaned up the glass and put the brooms away. Then I walked toward the kitchen. "What you got to eat in this joint? Almost dying twice makes a brotha hungry."

"I got a couple of T-bones in the freezer. I'll thaw them out in the microwave and light up the grill."

"Cool."

Jesse grabbed the steaks out of the freezer and put them on a plate in the microwave. "Shit, Dude, I can't believe my T.V. broke. A rat probably chewed through one of the television wires and fucked up the system. Dirty motherfuckers."

Jesse closed the microwave door, punched in five minutes on the timer, and pushed Start. I leaned back against the countertop. Suddenly a hissing sound grabbed my attention. "Shhh … Man, you hear that?"

"Hear what, man?" Jesse asked.

"That hissing noise."

"Now that you mention it, yeah."

"It sounds like its coming from the stove under the microwave." I said. We quietly stared at each other.

Suddenly, the microwave makes a high-pitched squeal like the T.V. We slowly backed away. The microwave door explodes, igniting a fireball from the gas off the stove. We cowered for cover. A roaring fire shot from the range, and smoke quickly filled every inch of the room.

Jesse screamed in a bitch ass voice, "Oh, Lord!!!"

"You all right, man! You okay?" I screamed, trying to see him through the thick smoke.

"Yeah! Yeah! Get the fire extinguishers in the cabinet by your feet!"

I tossed a fire extinguisher to Jesse, and we quickly put out the fire. I cut off the gas from the stove. Covered in meat, our extinguishers empty, we collapsed to the floor.

I wiped off my face, "Shit, did you inspect the house before you moved in, Dude?"

"Yeah, the motherfucker checked out tip-top. I don't understand what's going on."

"Oh, I think you've angered the Booty Gods," I said thoughtfully.

"What, you think one of my dips had something to do with this?"

"Dude, have you fucked yourself retarded? What do you think? Any of your dips know how to hotwire shit? Any of you dips know carpentry? Any of your dips mad at you right now? Or does this shit happen every Friday night! Tell me so I can buy tickets for the next show! What's next, the fucking house gonna crack in half, or what maybe the ground will open up and swallow this big bitch whole with us in it?"

Suddenly the kitchen wall cabinets fell down, collasping onto the sink and floor. The plates, glasses, and silverware crashed onto the floor behind us.

Jessie scoots away from the dishes, "Fuck! I betcha it was that bitch Sonja."

"Duh, do ya think? What you gonna do?"

Jesse hopped up, "I'm about to go over that ho's house and fuck her shit up. I'm gonna take her bike and dump it into that lake."

"And you'll be disbarred too. Go upstairs, calm down, and we'll figure out what to do."

Jesse slammed his fist into a wall, "Naw, fuck her, that fuckin' bitch!" Jesse stormed out the kitchen. "She wanna fuck up my shit, I'm gonna kill that bitch!"

I grabbed Jesse's arm. I wanted to kick his black ass for getting me in this shit, but I knew that this fool needed me, "Calm your ass down before you fuck your life away."

"Naw! Fuck that Spic!"

"Jesse, calm down, or I'm gonna knock your ass out! I'm not gonna let you do something you are gonna regret. Go upstairs and calm your ass down."

"A'ight Man, I'm gonna take a shower and cool my head off."

"I'll walk you up."

I followed behind Jesse, who took baby steps to the bathroom. He looked like he was scared to walk on the floor patterns because any of them could be a booby trap. We got upstairs, and he slowly opened the bathroom door. His hand shook as he felt for the light switch in the dark room. He flicked it on and cowered in paranoid fear. He looked the bathroom up and down, turning on the shower, took off his shirt, and looked in the mirror. He walked over to the tub and tried to open the drain but the lever was stuck.

"What a night, what a fuckin' night! Damn! Shit the drain is closed."

"Let me help you out." I pulled on it hard, but I was unable to make it budge. "Let me go get a wrench."

"In the kitchen under the sink," he said, turning off the faucet. Suddenly music sounds above the tub. We curiously looked up at the ceiling.

"What is that?" I asked and stared harder at the ceiling. "Is that Sade?"

"Yeah I know that song, that's 'Is It a Cri … ' " A crack crawled quickly across the ceiling. Without notice, a large boom box crashed through ceiling into the full tub below. The lights flickered on and off as I crouched down and covered my head.

"Oh my god … oh my god … oh my god … this bitch is trying to kill me."

"Jesse, Jesse! You okay, man!"

I stood up to see this punk ass sitting in a ball in the corner and rocking back and forth. My mouth dropped as I watched the radio sizzle in the bathtub, igniting sparks on the floor.

"Jesse, Jesse, Jesse, snap out of it, man! Come on we're leaving before Sonja fricassees your goofy ass. Where're your keys?"

"I … I … I don't know. Uh … Oh … G … G … G … God … O … On … On the patio, I think."

I helped Jesse up and we carefully walked through the house to the patio door.
"There're my keys, man."

We stepped out onto the patio and heard a large creaking sound. We slowly backed into the kitchen. A cloud of dust raced across the deck as it started to break apart from the house. I watched in shock as large pieces of wood fell into the trees below. Jesse slammed his fist into a wall. I looked down and noticed inches above the floor a thin tripwire inches above the floor we must have disturbed.

"Fuck! Fuck! Fuck! This bitch has thoroughly fucked up my house! I can't believe this shit!" Jesse fell to the floor and started to weep liked a binky-less baby.

I just looked down at the trees below. Looks like The Booty Gods had just taken a sacrifice.

In the truck, Kyle stares dumbfounded at me, "So what happened after that?"

"Well then things started to get ugly. We called the police. Jesse filed a complaint against Sonja, and they had their day in court. She got off scott-free. They couldn't prove how Sonja could have gotten into the house and did all this damage, especially, since Jesse just moved in and spent practically the entire week at home getting everything ready. He even worked at home that week so she would have had to done it while he was there. It would have been impossible for her to gut out this house while he was in it. But somehow, I know it was her. I don't how she did it, but somehow that bitch did it. She knows I know, but I just can't prove it."

"That is some deep shit, man, deep."

"For sho. Damn here's Channel 10. I hope old girl is here."

"What we gonna say to her?"

"I don't know. I'll think of something."

CHAPTER SEVEN

THE WRATH
SONJA

I couldn't believe I saw Xavier's fine ass today. Damn, it seems like its been about a year. I always liked him, he seemed a real man, not like that punk ass Jessie. Now, I'm not making any excuses for what I did, but that bitch had it coming. I just hate that X got caught up in the middle of dat shit. I should have been trying to get with him in the first place. Well, there's no chance of that now. Shit, I never wanted to be one of those sour ass women who hate all men, but a brother like Jesse makes a bitch give up on the dick and charge up her vibrator. If I didn't have to go to work and if Xavier didn't turn down six streets to avoid me, I might try to give some type of half-assed apology. But shit who am I kidding? That ain't ever gonna happen. Even though he won't admit it, Xavier knows Jesse had it coming to him.

A year ago, I went over Jesse's house dressed up in a French maid outfit. You know how hard it is to drive on a motorcycle in a French maid outfit wrapped in a leather trench coat in the middle of July? But when you're in love, you don't care, and stupidity doesn't exist. Anyway, I go over there and call him on the phone. I wanted to make sure that I broke that habit of just stopping by cause I knew it annoyed him. Really, I forgot until I got to the house. I called from the driveway, but there wasn't an answer. I knew he had to be home because both his cars were there. I called again, no answer. I waited about ten minutes and no answer, so I drove around the back just to make sure I wasn't about to miss him. Shit, I already rode halfway across town with my ass out so I might as well check before I leave without getting some.

I pulled up on my bike in the alley to see if he was chillin' on the deck. I called again just to make sure, and he finally picked up. He said it was at the job, so I said okay even though he was actin' funny. I got ready to turn around when I heard screams coming from one of the houses on the hill above. I was hoping, that it wasn't his. But in my heart I knew. We always know deep down inside,

even if we tell and beg ourselves for it not to be true.
We know if our lover is cheating. I had to be sure; I
had to see it with my own eyes. I pulled up a little
ways from the house and got off my bike. I shivered
all over as I saw Jesse and dat ho Melissa on the back
patio. I just had lunch with that bitch yesterday. We
sisters in the same damn sorority! Ever the ho, I
shouldn't have been surprised.

I couldn't move as I felt my coat was
blowing in the wind around me. I know I looked like
a damn fool, standing there dressed in a French maid
outfit for anyone to see, but I was stuck, frozen in
pain. It was like I was just stabbed a thousand times
at the sight of him smiling and screamin' how good
she was. I wanted to run up and kill him for ripping
my heart out. But I had something better in store.

Three days passed. I didn't eat, I didn't sleep,
I couldn't do anything but think of those two on the
deck. I meditated in my apartment for hours trying to
get the nerve to do what I had to do. I calmed my
spirit. Thunder rumbled outside as I looked that the
clock; eleven o' clock, almost midnight. I had my bag
already packed. I went and took a long hot shower
and put on my yellow <u>Kill Bill</u> body suit, complete

with red lace thong panties and no bra. I wanted him
to see my nipples poking through the suit. I wrapped
my hair in a tight bun. I walked over to the full-
length mirror and stared at myself for what seemed to
be forever.

Thunder rumbled again. I shook off the daze
and put on my leather gloves and high heel boots
which I always made me feel ten feet tall. Thunder
crashed again, followed by lightening. The power
went out and I started to panic. I hate thunderstorms.
Ever since I was a kid, they scared the shit out of me.
In the dark, I inhaled and exhaled and calmed myself.
I thought about all the nights I made love to him. All
the secrets I shared, all the love I gave, waiting on
him hand and foot, being his maid, cook, best friend,
and private whore. I thought about all the times he
claimed to love me but was too scared because his
heart had already been broken. I ignored the rumors
about him stickin' his two-inch dick in any bitch with
a pulse. I pretended it didn't matter, I was ready to
give up having orgasms for the rest of my life to be
with him because I thought his heart could satisfy me
in ways that his stump of a dick couldn't. In the back
of my mind, I knew he was playing me, but I was in

love; I thought I could change him. I thought I could teach him love. Now I would teach him vengeance.

The lights came on my room as I stood in front of my mirror. I looked into my eyes and walked to my bed. My heels clicked on the hardwood floor, my stomach burned, and my heart was dead. I felt empowered.

I grabbed my bag and hopped on my bike. Rain poured as I started the engine and jetted onto the street. Not even the thunder would stop me.

It was 2:00 A.M. and that bastard stumbled to the door. I played the naughty roll seducing him on the couch. I made sure he wanted me. I slipped over to the bar and poured him a shot glass of Brandy. Brandy was one of the only dark liquors he would drink so it perfectly concealed the crushed sleeping pills I put in his drink. Jessie always had a problem sleeping so he would take either a sleeping pill or a stiff drink to relax. I knew with both, he'd be out for hours. I put the envelope holding the powder underneath the bottle, and soon as he downed the Brandy I knew he was mine. We made love, no we fucked, and as usual he passed out in his room.

I crept over to the bedroom door and peeped in to see if he was sleep. He was snoring hard. I walked over to the bar and washed out Jesse's shot glass. Underneath the bottle of Brandy, I took out the small envelope, crumbled it up, and wet a paper towel to wipe away the powder that fell from the envelope. I washed out the envelope and put it in my purse. I took a swig and walked over to my clothes on the floor. Soon I found myself outside in front of my bike, grabbing a large duffle from the seat. I looked around and carried the bag inside, dropping it on the floor. I reached down and pulled out a baggie with a pair of panties in it. I assumed they were Melissa's; I didn't give a fuck. I walked into Jessie's room and stood over him. He was still snoring.

"How could you let me find these in the bed we made love in so many times? You Bastard!" I slapped him, but he didn't budge. "I would have given anything for you." I slapped him again and began to cry. He continued to snore. Watching him sleep broke my heart again. He didn't give a damn, so why should I?

I went into the living room and pulled out a drill. I wrapped my hair up and changed into all black. I pulled the hood on my shirt over my head, grabbed the bag, and headed for his prized T.V. and began to drill. I moved like a shadow in the night through the pitch-black house. I felt like a ghost outside myself, like a wraith looking for revenge. I worked all night.

Finally I packed my bag and pulled off the hood. I took the panties out of the bag and placed them in the middle of the floor. Under the rising sun, I left shutting the door and that part of my life behind me.

I have to admit that at times I felt bad about what I'd done, especially since last I heard Jesse was checked into Arnead Mental Hospital after that. But fuck him. What I really feel bad about is Xavier being caught in the middle. I'd feel terrible if he had of gotten hurt. I don't think I could have lived with that. Someday, I'll have to try to make that up to him. But I'll say this, for as wrong as it was, and as crazy as it was, I truly savored that ass whuppin'.

CHAPTER EIGHT

THE STUDIO
XAVIER & KYLE

Kyle and I get out of the truck and head toward the Channel 10 Studio building. I'm nervous, I don't know what I'm gonna say. I'm pessimistic that she'll pull the story but miracles happen, and today is the day for one. We open the door to the studio building; this place was huge, big time. Kyle pans over the elegant interior as I walk up to the receptionist's desk. Kyle follows behind checking out all the secretaries in the office.

"May I help you?" the receptionist asks.

"Hey, how are you? My name is Xavier Thompson, and this is my brother Kyle. We are with the office of Michael Thompson."

Kyle's horny ass interrupts, eyeing the receptionist up and down, "What up cutie. How you doin'?"

The receptionist smiles, I roll my eyes and ask, "Excuse me, is Miss Gomez in?"

"Yes, she is but she's in Editing. Can I take a message?"

Kyle smiles confidently. "Could I trouble you to disturb her? It is of an urgent matter."

The receptionist flirtatiously giggles, "Well, I could try and page her."

"Well, thank you, beautiful," Kyle says, working his magic.

"You're very welcome." We walk away from the desk and sit in the waiting room. Kyle looks over at the receptionist and winks. She smiles and looks away as we whisper to each other.

Kyle licks his lips. "Man, check out the titties on her."

"Dude, focus," I say in an attempt to control him.

"I am. I'm focused on those titties."

"Would you forget the titties."

"Tell me you don't like those titties."

"The titties are nice, but we are not here for titties. It's not titty time now. No titties."

"No titties?"

"Not even a tit."

"A'ight. A'ight."

Muzak plays overhead as I look around the lobby and focus on another girl walkin' with a switch to a room in the back. I look out the corner of my eye and notice Kyle is rubbing his upper thigh and crouch. My eyes widen. I think this freak about to jack off!

I nudge his arm, "What are you doin'?"

"Check out the back piece on that bird."

"No ass, titties, gams, yams, boobs, dirty pillows, muffins, back pieces, pies, thighs, or eyes. Come on Man concentrate, shit."

"A'ight Man."

Kyle sighs and places his hands on his head. I nervously rub a spot off my pants leg.

Kyle snaps his fingers, "You know who I saw the other day?"

"Hmmm?"

"Mrs. Jennkins."

"Really? Where you see her?"

"Kroger, and baby got an ass on her."

I shift in my chair, "Dude, which Mrs. Jennkins you talking about?"

"Geraldine."

"Our grandmomma?!"

"She not our grandmomma by blood; she our step-grandmomma."

This nigga's a freak. "Kyle, she's eighty six … with rickets."

"She still got a lot of ass. I saw her shaking that ass in the grocery store. She got a mean switch on her."

"Yeah, I bet the plastic hip and cane help."

Kyle sucks his teeth. "I bet her mama got ass too."

"Kyle … her mama would be like a hundred and twenty … you fuckin' freak Dude. You need religion or some coochie or something Man. Between our brother wearing panties and you wanting to screw everything born in this century, I'm the only normal one in the lot of us."

"Man, you got some freak in you too. Dude. I know."

Theresa finally walks out into the waiting room. Damn, I can't believe how fine she is. I've seen her on T.V, but damn! I don't know if it's just because I'm on my way to becoming a born again virgin or what, but, shit, she looks good as hell. She's got a statuesque, refined beauty that make a Dude wanna turn in his playa card. If she wasn't trying to ruin my brother's career, I might have to holla at her. A glare from her thin wire frame glasses brings me out of the trance about her hourglass body and silky, confident walk.

We rise as Theresa shakes our hands. "Gentlemen, I'm Theresa Gomez. How can I help you?"

"Yes, my name is Xavier Thompson, and this is my brother Kyle. We're with the office of Michael Thompson. Is there somewhere we can talk in private?"

"Of course, of course. Please come back to my office."

Theresa leads us to her office. She looks as good from the back as she does from the front. She sits down behind a huge desk as we sit in the guest chairs in front of it.

Theresa pushes a button the intercom, "Sarah please page my extension after five minutes unless Mr. Jennison from CNN calls."

Sarah answers on the other end, "Yes, Theresa. Five minutes."

"Hmm, CNN. Big story?" I ask.

"No, big opportunity. I've just accepted an offer to be one of their new evening anchors."

"Well, congratulations."

"Thank you, I'll be leaving the station next week. Can I offer you something to drink?"

"No thank you," I reply staring at her cleavage about to bust out of her tight blue blazer. She caught me looking, her eyes going from my eyes to her breasts back to my eyes. "So, how can I help you handsome boys today?" She asks.

I cross my legs, trying to play it cool even though I would have loved to pick her up and hit it right there on the desk. "It has come to my attention that you are planning to air a special report about Mr. Thompson on your news broadcast tonight?"

"That's right, we're planning to run a special piece on Mr. Thompson tonight. Why, is there a problem?"

"Well would you mind telling is the subject of the piece?"

"I'm sorry. I usually keep exclusive rights to my stories. I don't reveal any aspects of my exposés because there's a lot of competition in my business, and I have a strict policy of confidentially until airtime. Is there any specific reason for your concern?"

"We just want to make sure that he is seen in fair and impartial light and that any matters of his personal life that do not have a bearing on his public policy are kept personal."

"Hmmm, how so Xavier?"

"May I be frank?"

"By all means."

"I know that you stumbled upon my brother in a very compromising and embarrassing position."

"I suppose you could say that." She smiles slightly.

"Well we feel that this is a position that the public does not need to be exposed to. Is there any way that your report could not reflect him in that private and rare moment?"

Kyle injects. "Mr. Thompson can really make a positive change in this community; a change that is a long time coming. We would hate to see that change not happen because of a temporary moment of embarrassment."

Theresa places her hands together in a prayer-like fashion. "Well, I agree Mr. Thompson could indeed be an asset to this area, especially in the Brown and Black community, but I cannot short change the truth."

I uncross my legs and lean forward. "I'm not asking you to shortchange the truth. Just focus on his campaign platform."

"I simply feel that we have a difference of opinion. I feel that all aspects of our leaders' lives are open for discussion, especially if those aspects reveal something about their moral fiber. Besides, as much as I may like Mr. Thompson, I have to remain impartial."

"We all get a little carried away, but it doesn't mean that everything he promises he won't deliver or he won't do everything in his power to serve the people in his district. Can't you cut him a break? Our office would greatly appreciate it."

Theresa takes off her glasses and places the tip of one of the frames in her mouth considering our plea.

Sarah buzzes in. "Five minutes, Theresa."

"I'm sorry, I'd like to help, but I have always been impartial and shared all aspects of my stories with my viewers. If the public wants to know, I'm committed to bring it to them. I'd like to help, but I can't. If you will excuse me, I have to get ready for tonight's show." She stands up.

We get up. I pull out my gold card case to hand her a business card, "If you reconsider, here's my card. Thank you for your time."

We leave the office defeated. I look back in the distance, trying to think of something more to say. I see Theresa sitting down at the desk, twirling my card in her fingers. She reads the card, stops for a moment, and then scrapes it across her chest. Maybe there is a shard of hope. She shakes her head, tosses the card in the trash, and leaves the room.

"Damn." I whisper to myself as we continued to leave the building. The walk back to the truck is slow and painful. The pride and purpose I felt before has soured to defeat and dejection.

Kyle sighs. "Well, that was a waste," he moans.

"I know, damn. She can do the report without exposing him. She's gotta be planning just to bust him out."

"You think she's in bed with Manning?"

"Could be, but I not getting that vibe. She seems like an opportunist. The story and scandal is what she cares about."

"I know, fuckin' ratings bitch. There's no point to embarrass him like this. Shit, what's next?"

We get in the truck. I place my head in my hands. "I don't know where to go now. I need to get something to eat. Let's go to the crib."

"A'ight."

We drive to my place, and things are pretty silent on the way. I kinda hope that it stays that way. Kyle always made fun of me because I am sort of a neat freak. Everything has to be in place. Frankly, I'm not in the mood for his mouth today.

We get out the truck. I grab my backpack, and check the mail as Kyle walks up the stairs to my place. Jennifer, my neighbor, waves to me as she hops in her ride. She must be on the way to get to the gym or something, dressed in a little tube top. As soon as I saw her come out her apartment I damn near expected Kyle to tackle her and start humpin' her leg, but he walks past her without noticing her. He must be worried.

Kyle looks at the apartment and shakes his head, "Man, I need to take a shower."

"Still got grease up your ass, Man? I can't believe you running around downtown with your dick swinging in the wind, looking like the poster boy for Astroglide."

"It was your damn idea."

"A'ight, a'ight, you right, Man."

"I'm going take a shower."

"A'ight, you want something to eat?"

"Yeah Man, hook me up."

Kyle grabs some towels out of the linen closet. I knew exactly what was next. He shakes his head at the perfectly symmetrically stacked towels in the closet. He walks into the bathroom.

"Dude you have got to be the cleanest Negro in Indy. What's this?" Kyle screams. Aw shit here we go. I walk over to see what he is talking about.

Kyle bends down and notices my large tin box. "Oh, no you didn't," he says as he reaches in the box and pulls out a disposable toilet seat cover. "Aw, Dude, what the hell you got about six, seven replacement boxes?"

"Yeah, so?"

"How many are in a box?"

"Uh … 100 seat covers in each."

"Dude, you got some issues."

"What?"

"What? Look at this!" Kyle opens my bleach cabinet. "What's up with this?"

"That's my bleach cabinet."

"Bleach cabinet?"

"Yeah, you heard me."

"Dude most people got maybe a bottle of bleach. You got a 'bleach cabinet'? There's like two, three dozen of bottles of beach in here." He closes it and opens another cabinet.

"What the hell, Man? You got what, fifty tubes of bathroom cleanser?"

"What?"

Kyle leaves the bathroom and walks across the hall and opens my other linen closet. It is stocked only with Lysol spray, hundreds of cans.

"X Man, why you got some much damn Lysol and bleach? You cuttin' up bodies and shit in here?"

"Nah, Man the bathroom gotta be clean."

Kyle sits down at the breakfast bar in the kitchen as I get a frying pan from below.

"Well, how many damn bathrooms you got, shit?"

"One."

"Then why you got so much bleach?"

"Bathroom gotta be clean, Dude. What ain't you understanding?"

"Are you running hoes or an orphanage in here at night or something?"

"No, the bathroom just has to be clean." I opened up the fridge. "Shit, between Mike's panties, and your greased up ass I forgot to go shopping."

"You got about four hundred and ninety-seven bottles of bleach in yo crib and no food? What kinda sense that make?"

"Man, you just ain't understanding," I grouse.

"You right about that shit."

"Come on, get something out the closet to put on and we'll go to Mike's."

"Cool." Kyle leaves to change clothes.

"And keep you greasy ass out my suits!!"

"I ain't gonna be too many more greasy ass jokes!"

"Just shut up and come on!"

CHAPTER NINE

I FEEL SO FREE WITH

YOU

XAVIER

We pull up to Michael's driveway. My stomach feels knotted like a pretzel, seeing Michael run out his house with a smile so bright like it was midnight I could see it two blocks away. He steps out to my truck. Shit, what am I gonna say to this Dude?

Michael comes around the front of the truck. He taps the hood gleefully with his fist. "My Boy! My Boy! What happened! Tell me, how'd you put the smack down on her! Talk slow, what happened? Is she pullin' the story?"

Kyle gets out of the truck and heads straight to the house. "She didn't budge. I'm going to get some food."

Michael turns to Kyle and then back to me, "What …what happened?"

"She was sayin' some crap about how she couldn't short change the truth, and she always stands behind her ethics."

"Ethics?! She has the ethics of backwater pimp!" I jump when Michael smacks his fist into his hand. "Damnit, I can't believe this shit! Two years of fuckin' work destroyed in one minute! Fuck!"

I put my arm around Michael's shoulder. "We're not down and out yet. I promise you, I'll figure something out."

Michael jerks away. "What? What, man, what can we do? As soon as the Urban Christian League finds out about this, there is no way we'll get their support. Without their backing, it's a done deal."

"Just calm down and let's think about this."

"Think about what?! Its over. I know her type. She's got a scandal in hand, and she's runnin' with it. Damn it! I might as well call the headquarters and let them know."

Michael turns his back to walk into the house. I feel so bad for him. I'm trying to come up with the words, any words, that will help.

"Look the speech ain't until tomorrow … ."

Just then a beat up car pulls into the driveway. Michael takes off his glasses and rubs his eyes. "Damn, what now? Another damn reporter? Man, I can't deal with this. Get rid of them, Xavier." Michael starts to open the front door to the house.

"I don't think this is a reporter, man. Look."

A voice cries from the tinted windows from the car, "Excuse me Mr. Thompson? Michael Thompson?"

Michael turns around, looking curiously at the shabby, rust covered car as it backfires in the driveway. A frail looking woman steps out of the car and walks up to the porch.

"I'm sorry to interrupt, Mr. Thompson. Can I talk to you for a second?"

"Well ... su ... sure how can I help you?"

"I'm sorry to bother you. I saw you on my way to school, and I had to stop. I was hoping you could help me out. My name is Shelly Harrison. I see you on T.V. all the time talking about your campaign for the people and the end of business as usual."

"Yeah ... ."

"Well, Mr. Thompson, I'm at the end of my rope. I've been to City Hall, the Housing Authority, even to the police station, and no one is listening to me. I don't know what to do?"

Shelly wipes away a tear. Michael gently grabs her arm, "Please come sit down. This is my brother Xavier. What can we do?"

We sit on the porch. Shelly wipes another tear, "The problem is that I moved to an apartment on the East side. At the time I signed my lease, I was nine months pregnant. My husband abandoned us, so I had to get a place quick. The rent was good, and everything seemed okay. Well, one day I went out shopping with my son and came home and found one of the maintenance men in my apartment watching T.V. and eating a sandwich. I asked him what he was doing there, and he said that he was replacing a coil in the refrigerator. I told him that I didn't put in a call to maintenance and would appreciate some advance notice before someone comes in my home. He said, 'We don't need to give you shit,' and left. I went down to complain to the landlord, and she said that in the lease I signed that it said that apartment staff can come in the apartment at any time day or night without notice. Plus they said that if they are refused entry into the apartment there is a five hundred fee. Five hundred dollars! I can't afford that, I can't. That's more than the rent!"

Kyle brings his horny ass to the storm door. "Damn, she fine! Hey Girl what's up? What yo name is?"

I smack the storm door with my fist and point for Kyle to get out. He knew I wasn't playin' so he turns right around. He probably thought I was trying to hit myself.

"Okay you were sayin'?" I ask.

"Well, recently one of the other tenants got a seven hundred dollar cable bill. Somebody had ordered thirty days of pay per view porn. We went to the police but they just told us a fill out a report and they'll look into it. The other day I came out the shower and the maintenance man was there to fix a loose door hinge. I didn't ask for this. There wasn't a damn thing wrong with the door. I have no idea what to do. Everywhere I go a door is slammed in my face, and I can't afford to pay for a lawyer. I went to legal aid, but it will be months before they can get to me, and the lawyer just told me to buy a gun. I have a newborn! I can't wait for one of them to do God knows what to us. I don't know where to go."

I look over at Michael. He is standing up and beginning to pace. I knew the wheels are turning.

Michael was like the freakin' John Shaft of Indy. When it came down to putting ghetto ass whoopin' on somebody, Michael was a fuckin' surgeon; especially when it came to somebody taking advantage of a female, a single mom at that. I knew Mike was about to get in dat ass.

Michael stops pacing and rubs his chin. "Don't you worry about nothing. I got you. I'm gonna talk to someone at county clerk's office, and I know a couple of investigators downtown that will definitely be down."

I look at Shelly and say, "I know a couple of detectives with the Sheriff's office that owe me a favor. Now, that I think about it I can talk to Smitty at City Hall and pull a few strings."

Michael snaps his fingers. "In fact, what about Mrs. Hanson's boys Shaka n' Lil' Darryl?"

"Who? Oh, yeah, you talking about the two 290 pound brothers at the gym?"

"Yeah, exactly. They two of my boxers at the gym I coach. Shelly, I think you about to adopt two little brothers. Now they ain't gonna do nothing illegal, but I guarantee you the maintenance men ain't gonna be poppin' up in your place unannounced no mo.'"

This is classic Michael. He is the only brotha I know that can get politicians, preachers, and back alley brothas together for tha' cause.

"You come down to 909 Meka lane first thing tomorrow morning, and we gonna light a blowtorch under their butts."

I smile. "By time we're through with them they'll be afraid to even draft a lease."

"Thank you! Thank you! I'll stop by tomorrow. 909 Meka lane?"

Michael takes out a business card. "Right 909 Meka lane. Keep this on the D.L. I want to launch a surprise attack against these kats. We'll discuss a battle plan tomorrow."

"Thank you, Mr. Thompson. Thank you." Shelly walks back to her car and takes off.

"You see that man! You see Mike! That's what's it's about. Puttin' the smack down on some wicked kats, man! That's why you can't drop out! You can make a difference; we can make a difference, man. First this slum lord, then Manning, then who knows. I'm not letting you drop out. You need to concentrate on that speech tomorrow. Fuck a Theresa Gomez! Give me a little more time to think of something! A'ight, Dude!"

"A'ight, man. Let's get something to eat, and we'll put our heads together."

We go inside and Michael cooks breakfast over the stove as I get some juice out the fridge. Kyle walks out of the bathroom, "Now, you see this Negro normal. Mike, you seen this Dude's bathroom?"

Michael gets some pots out of the cabinet, "You mean the two hundred bottles of bleach and soft scrub."

I sit down and pour Kyle a glass of juice.

Kyle sips the orange juice and grabs a piece of toast, "Man, that shit ain't normal."

"You ain't seen the blowtorch," Michael says with a frown.

"Blowtorch?"

"Hell yeah, blowtorch!"

"Aw, come on now, what ya'll talking about this for at the breakfast table."

"Kyle, you know why he carries that bag all the time?"

"Naw, why?"

"You ain't know!?"

I grab Mike's wrist, "Come on, Dude. Don't get his ass started on this shit."

Mike pulls away laughing. "This little bitch carries around small blowtorch and a case of baby wipes soakin' in bleach everywhere he goes."

Kyle laughs. "Come on man, I know he lying on you, dawg. I know he is."

Debra walks by the trio. "Yep, tell 'em about Auntie Gloria's picnic at the park."

"Where the hell did you come from? Aw…come on man. How about them Colts this year, huh?" I ask, trying to change the subject. they may go to the Super Bowl, huh?"

Michael sits down. "This Dude goes and eats Auntie Vern's potato salad. You know Vern keeps a nasty house … "

I had to but in because Michael ain't gonna tell it right, "Yeah…yeah…so after a half hour my stomach starts bubbling up. I'm making a pot of chili in my guts, and I run to the port-a-potty … "

At the park, I flung open the door to the port-a-potty, at the same time holding the back of my damn pants with one hand in an attempt to hold in the fury bubbling inside   and my black bleach bag in the other. I went in there, and, man, it was like Hell took a shit. So I ran out, but my stomach is still making chili. So I ran back in, but I looked down at the seat and ran back out. I buckled and dashed back into the potty, grabbing the back of my pants.

I opened the bag and pulled out a spray bottle of bleach. Yeah I got a damn spray bottle of bleach too! Anyway I sprayed the toilet all over. Seconds later, I took out another spray bottle of bleach and sprayed both in all directions. The potty rocked back and forth and the door flung open, and I see couple of kids passing by stop and stare at me. "Mind yo business!" I told the little brats and slammed the door. I reached in the bag and took out my small blowtorch and bottle of cologne. I dropped the bag, poured the cologne on the seat, ignited the torch, and snarled bending over the toilet."

Kyle drops his fork in disbelief, "Xavier, you set the toilet on fire?"

"Yeah, fire kills everything."

"And this is normal to you?" he asks.

"Yeah, what the problem is?"

"The problem is I went in after yo goofy ass came out," Michael says.

"Well, this was some horrendous Son of Satan, devil dog shit. I mean if shit, shit out shit, then that is what this shit was. I had to leave."

"So I go in the potty to do my business, and this bitch got the toilet seat on fire. I mean Fire! Not fire but *Fire*! This fool has the seat so hot the hairs on my ass singed.

I sat down in that stankin' ass bathroom and thought I was gonna die. The port-a-potty was rocking crazy. I was screamin' inside, all type of fucks and bitches. Next thing you know motherfuckin' port-a-potty falls over with me in it! I could have killed you!"

Michael lays down some plates and serves Kyle and me breakfast. He sits down at the table, and we begin to eat breakfast. "So I got bleachy shit all over me, and this asshole is running to go shit in the fucking lake."

Kyle slaps the table laughing, "Naw, naw, naw, I'll top that. Did you tell Mike about Pam?"

I drop my fork. "Kyle, Michael, what we gonna do about this tape? I think we can…"

"Naw, Dude! Don't change the subject, man. Tell me about Pam."

"Where's yo wife anyway? Debra! Maybe she has some ideas about the situation."

Kyle and Michael laugh. "He still trying to change the subject. You gonna tell it or you want me to?" Kyle asks.

"Come on, man, spill it!" Kyle says rubbing his chin.

"A'ight shit. Pam was this new secretary in the office. She was…"

Michael rubs his hands together and asks, "What she look like?"

"About 5'10, 140-150 lbs. Real skinny, no tits at all but she had a back piece on her. Easily a four to five hander, which looked real good on a chick her size, man. At any rate, she was a new secretary at the office…"

Things were pretty busy in the office that morning. We were handling a huge case getting ready to file charges against Peter Phillis, that big contractor on the south side. So I'd been swamped all day. I'm standing at the copy machine talking to a couple of the guys in Collections, and Pam walked by. She got our attention real quick, bending down to open a drawer full of files.

My boy Kurt walked past her and meets us at the copier, "X dawg, look at the wagon she draggin'."

"I know, Kurt. Hmm …I know man. I know. Damn."

"That's the new girl, ain't it? What's her name?"

"That's Pam, one of the new secretaries in Cold Files."

Pam got up and walked by the men at the copiers. She smiled and headed back to her cube. Simultaneously, we all looked down as she switched away, enjoying the attention. I knew she was. Another Dude walked past her and turned around bumping in a file cabinet besides him. I knew she was eatin' this shit up!

Kurt brushed his goatee. "She skinny as hell but got ass on her. Damn."

I smiled, "She got a grade A. ass on her. That's good butt. Big and shaped right. That's good butt."

"That's enough onion to keep a man in tears for a week. She working it too."

"Oh, she knows we lookin."

"I don't give a damn. She got a man?" Kurt asks.

"Supposedly, she's dating a pro-basketball player, but she don't act like it. She is a notorious flirt."

"Man, that don't mean shit. All women do that. Its like they get off on making a brotha pant for it."

"And our dumb asses fall for that shit every single time. Let me get back to it, man. I'll catch you later," I said as I walked away from the copier.

I walked down the hall, and Pam got up and walked in the opposite direction towards me. She eyed me up and down as she passed. I turned around and smiled checking her out on the way back to the office. Damn, I ain't never seen cotton look so good.

Later that afternoon, I was typing on my computer, when a knock on the door distracted me. I turned around to see Pam.

"Excuse me, Mr. Thompson?"

"Yes?"

"Mr. Doobson asked me to run these files over to you for your review."

"Thank you, ummmm?"

"Pamela, Pam Vera."

I stood up and shook Pam's hand. "You just started recently, right?"

"Yep, just a couple of weeks ago."

"So, how do you like it, so far?"

"It's cool, a lot of stuffy suits in this office. But it's cool, a lot better than my old job."

"What was that?"

"Cleaning chitterlings at a meat market."

"What?" I asked incredulously.

"Yep. But the bonus was all the free chitterlings I could eat."

"Are you serious?" I asked, dumbfounded with her revelation.

"Naw, I'm just playin'."

We laughed as I took a quick look up and down. Pam noticed but played it off.

"So, Pam, are you new to town?"

"Yeah, I'm originally from Matteson, Illinois."

"Really?! I'm from Chi-town! I know where Matteson is. I used to work there when I was in school. What brings you out here?"

"I got accepted to I.U. School of Dentistry."

"So you gonna be a dentist? That's why you got such a pretty smile?"

Pam giggled flirtatiously, "Thank you. I better get back to my files."

"All right, it was a pleasure to meet you."

"Oh, no the pleasure was definitely, all mine." Pam smiled as she looked me up and down.

She seductively walked away as I stared fixated on her butt. "Damn, she got a lot ass. Hmm, hamburger." I shook it off and started reading through the files…

At Michael's house, we continue to eat breakfast.

"So over the next few weeks, she'd come by the office and chit-chat, nothing big, but she's starting to get comfortable so she would do little shit to flirt."

"Like what?" Kyle asks.

"Pass by and smack my ass or rub her titties on my arm. She got like…what cup do women wear if they are flat?"

"That's an A cup." Michael answers.

"Well the chick is at A-1. So she was rubbing her tidnibbles on me, and I was hard as a rock. I have to admit it is something sexy about that shit. You know, the fact that you know and she knows what's going on but no else does. So anyway, a whole bunch of us went to lunch at the Hyatt and I found out the she's single, so I ask her out to dinner. She says, 'Yeah,' so first date is cool, second date is cool, and then comes the third date. Ya'll know my rule, something, a kiss, makin' out or something gotta happen on the third date. So I cook her to dinner at my place … ."

It was a cool night out as I looked out on the balcony slipping on a glass of Red. I had been working all day and finally my dinner was almost ready on the stove.

I'd hooked up some of my finest cuisine. I pulled out all the stops: lobster tail, asparagus tips, filet mignon, shrimp cocktail for to starters, and for dessert my seven layer chocolate cake. I had some Miles playin on the stereo. I was ready. Oh, man, I was ready for anythang.

The doorbell rang, I sprayed on a little cologne and checked myself in the mirror. I waited a minute before opening the door. I didn't want to seem too eager. Eventually I walked over to open the door. Pam stood outside, holding a bottle of wine.

"Hey, Big Daddy," she greets me.

"Hey, girl, how you doing? Come on in. Come on in, looking all good. Did you find the place okay?"

"I got turned around a bit, but it's all good. You looking good yourself. Here I brought a little wine for dinner."

I examined the bottle as she came in, "This is a good year. Where did you get this?"

"My uncle owns a vineyard in Nappa. He sends me bottles from time to time to sample. Dang, your place is immaculate for a bachelor."

I pulled out a seat for her in the kitchen. "Yeah I like everything in order. Please sit down."

"Such a gentleman, thank you." Pam giggled.

We sat down for a candlelight dinner. I have to admit I enjoyed her company and the electric vibe growing between us. She was pretty well versed and traveled; she seemed to have a pretty good head on her shoulders. Not like some of the chickenheads I'd had here in the past; talking about 'oh is this that filet min-none or what kind of ketchup you put in this scrimps sauce?' The last girl brought over some Kripple, Kool Aid, and Ripple for dinner. What the hell? Where do even get Ripple now a days?

Anyway, we quickly finished dinner and I got ready for dessert, which would seal the deal. My seven-layer cake would definitely get her ready for a nice calorie burning bedroom workout. Pam's mouth watered at the site of my decadent cake. I had her.

Pam took a bite and moaned, scraping the fork across her teeth. Her eyes rolled in the back of her head, "Hmm, God this is luscious. You are a fabulous chef. Where did you learn to cook?"

"Just watching my mom in the kitchen."

"Aww … How sweet. Hmmm, I gotta get a another piece."

Pam got up from the table and took our plates to the kitchen sink. I followed her to the sink biting my bottom lip at the site of her in her black chiffon pants that flow over her body like milk in a glass.

"Thanks, would you like another glass of wine?" I asked.

"I better not. I lose my inhibitions when I drink too much. I would hate to do something I'll regret in the morning being here with a strong, viral, Nubian…" Pam's fingernails grazed my upper arm. "…on second thought pour me another glass."

Pam giggled, looking me over as I poured another drink. This was turning out to be a great night! Pam walked into the living room and checked out my artwork on the wall.

"This is beautiful."

"Yeah, it is a Yvette Snow, a new artist in Indy."

"Aw, shoot check you out with the trophies!!!"

"I have a few."

"A few? There's about forty, forty-five."

"There's about fifty-seven," I proudly admitted.

"Wow, you should teach!"

"Yeah, I'm working on it."

"I did a little Taekwondo in college. I got to green belt."

"I'm impressed. Why'd you stop?"

"It was my last semester in school. I always thought about getting back into it. I'm still pretty flexible," she said and dropped to the floor in a full split.

"Damn, I see." My eyes started dancing.

"Yeah, the problem is getting back up." She laughed and reached her hand out to me. I grabbed it and pulled her up. "So, I guess you're quite the Renaissance man, huh? Fighter, excellent cook, fabulous since of style, and impeccable taste in music. I must say, I am impressed."

"And you ain't seen my real skills yet." I held my hand out and pulled her close to me.

"Oh really? Well, I'd love to see you in action…on and off the matt." She softly licked her lips and wrapped her hands around my shoulders.

"Oh I can *definitely* arrange a demonstration."

We slipped into a deep embrace. We made out in the living room for what seemed to be a half hour.

"Why don't you show me the rest of your place?" She suggested as she stroked the budge in the front of my pants. I picked her up and carried her to the bedroom. Against the bedroom door, our hands wandered over each other's body. Damn it felt good finally to grip that ass. She exhaled softly, ripping open my shirt and kissing down my neck, chest. Her warm breath sent send goose bump down my arms. Her lips were so soft my pecs started to budge trying to get closer to her. She started to flick her tongue on my nipples. That always drove me crazy. I think she could tell because she started to grind her waist against my throbbing shaft, exploring it with the velvet of her pants. I moaned as she tore open her shirt.

I slipped her on the bed and began my exploration of her body with my yearning lips. Her skin was velvet soft, with a slight caramel cream taste to it. I knew this wasn't gonna last too long. I could tell she couldn't wait either, the way she was pressing her entire body into mine as if I was a glass she wanted to pour herself into. I reached behind me to get a condom with one hand and unhook her bra with the other. I did even care if she had tidnibbles, I tried suckin' them anyway. She raised up and unbuttoned my pants. She took off her pants and panties. My nails gently grazed her back, rubbing her body up and down. She looked me over like a lioness savoring a hard fought meal and I was fully ready to surrender.

She leaned into my ear and whispered, "Boy, I'm about to give you some of the best pussy you will ever, ever find."

She slowly welcomed me into her intimacy. Clinching her walls around me, she screamed in delight. She placed her hand on my cheek, looking into my eyes. I knew I had found something special as I watched her body flow into mine … .

In Michael's kitchen, both Kyle and Michael begin to sweat. Kyle gulps down the rest of his juice as Michael reaches into the fridge and takes a gallon of water to the head.

Debra walks in, and looking at Michael asks, "What ya'll talking about in here?"

Michael wipes his mouth off, "I was just thinking of you, gal!"

"Hmm-huh. I know how you three are when you get together. Anyway, it's good to see you smile again. Well, I'm going to store, I'll meet you at campaign headquarters?"

"Yeah, we'll be there in a little bit."

"Don't worry, Baby. I'm sure everything will be just fine."

"I'm sure you're right, Baby." Michael says and gives Debra a kiss.

"I'll see ya'll in a little bit."

Michael slides over to the window.

"A'ight, she gone. You hittin' it and …"

"So yeah, I'm hitting it, and oh damn it was good. Definitely platinum, I mean Pla..ten..num. So we flip over and over and over, she's on top and starts grinding it. My eyes are all the way in the back of my head, my toes are cramped from curling. She hittin' it so good my head was tingling."

Kyle's mouth gapes open,."Tingling? Huh, aw shit!"

"For sho. This some of the best stuff I done had in a minute! It was so good I wanted to stop and write her a letter. It was so good that I was seeing rainbows, stars, the Lucky Charm's Leprechaun, blue moons, just all type of shit."

"Oh…Damn!" Michael and Kyle say simultaneously as they head for the fridge.

"You have no idea! She's riding it's like the last stallion out of town. I got my hands all over the five hander and I hear … "

In my room, Pam was panting hard and loud, riding me. I'm on the edge of sheer bliss.

"Oh…oh…God this is the best dick in the world!"

"Get it girl, get it!"

"Yes …Yes … I'm about to let loose! Yes!" Pam said gripping my shoulders.

"Do it girl! Do it!"

"Aw … shit! Shit! SHIT!!!" Pam leaned her head back and bit her bottom lip. Suddenly I heard a noise, like a balloon being deflated. I know I'm trippin' through; probably the punanny.

"You hear that?"

"What ?"

"Nothin', shit you feel good. It's so good I must be hearing thangs."

"Oh, I know, baby, I know. Just sit back and let me take it. I've been thinking about this dick all day!"

"Oh baby, it is yours!"

Pam grips my chest. "I know you gonna let me get some more of this tomorrow?"

"Oh … shit yeah…whenever you want it! Just don't stop!"

"I don't think I'm gonna be able to wait … ummmm oh shit…until tomorrow night. I think we need to take lunch in your office."

"Aw … shit … yeah … girl."

"Yes … yes say my name, say my fuckin' name!"

"Get it Pam! Get it PAM! Get it. PAM!"

"I'm cummin'! I'm cummin'! I'm cummin'! Aw Fuck!"

Pam holds her head back, my mouth opens wide, I'm almost there. Then it happened, that damn balloon sound again. Louder this time. Now, I ain't the smartest man, but I think this bitch just farted!

I held my breath thinking maybe it slipped out. She must have thought I liked it cause she did me the favor of fartin' again.

"Oh my God, are you making cheese. damn!"

Pam continued to ride me. "I just feel I can be so … so … so … "

Pam farts again. "… free with you. Keep your hands on my ass. I wanna cum again."

Pam grabbed my chest and pounced me hard. I held my breath and reached behind me to the headboard to get a bottle of cologne, but it kept slipping out of my hands. Maybe the Booty Gods were bored tonight.

"Get your big hands on my titties. Grabs those tits!"

What tittes? My eyes were starting to burn so I shut my eyes tight and patted Pam's chest looking for her breasts. I put two fingers together and flicked her nibblets. She must have liked that cause she farts again and had to audacity to try to moan loud to cover up the sound. I smacked my face trying to cover my nose.

Pam smiled, "Do you like it Baby?"

I uncovered my face to struggle to speak, "Yep ... so good ... oh yeah ... so good."

Pam grinds her waist hard against mine, "Oh, you feel so fuckin' good. Hmmm ... that was so good ... I need to take a shit."

What the Hell! Pam got up and seductively walked toward the bathroom. With every shake of her ass, she let out a baby fart.

She stopped and turned around at the doorway to the bathroom, "You keep that dick hard and up for me. When I come back I'm gonna bounce this big ass up the air and I want you to put my back out doggie style."

I held back the vomit churning in my stomach as Pam shut the bathroom door. I fell out of bed, frantically opening up my nightstand to pull out a cigar box full of incense sticks. Oh, this is some bull! I found a lighter and lit about thirty sticks at once, waving them like crazy in the air. I grabbed a can of Lysol and tried to empty it in air.

Aw, fuck this! I put the lighter to the Lysol can and shot out a stream of fire in the air. I emptied the can and grabbed the incense sticks again waving them all over. I came to the bathroom door and stopped in horror.

I listened at the door and this bitch is birthin' a fuckin' cow in there. She droppin bombs like Baghdad and moanin' the whole time like this is making her cum again. So I heard a flush and figured she was done. But oh no. Round two! Water splashed in the bathroom like she was joggin' on the beach. I'm fighting to remain conscious. I was about to die butt naked; my dick is linguini! Armageddon is happening in my bathroom! I'm blessing the door with the incense, trying to exorcise this big ass, shit monster out of my house when the toilet flushes again. I hopped back in the bed. Pam finally came out of bathroom,

"Oh God, hmmm, damn that cheese."

I put my hand over my mouth to keep my dinner down.

"Oh damn, I think I'm a size four again. Whew," Pam said as she walked toward me.

I threw the covers over my face as Pam smiled rubbing her stomach. "I wouldn't go in there for about ten, fifteen minutes, if you know what I'm sayin'? Hmmmmm, I hope you kept that dick hard because I'm about to smack your balls with this ghetto booty."

I was bout to throw the fuck up watching Pam's sultry walk to the window with a damn line of toilet paper hangin out her ass! I turned my face into the pillow and just wanted to die. Lord, take me now!

"Oh, baby, let me open up a window. Shit, I think you gave me the B.G.'s."

Pam looked over at me lying in bed. She slinked up to the bed pulls back the covers. She turned her back to me and had to nerve to say, "Hmmmm, .let me sit on your face, Baby."

I felt my eyes about to jump out my head. I coughed, "Oh, naw, why don't you let me get it for a while?"

"Oh, Baby, I want you to focus on this ass. How 'bout I give you a show and ride it backwards?"

I could only focus on the toilet paper hanging out of her ass as she sits on my lap and moans.

I closed my eyes tight. We've gotten this far, so I figured I'm gonna man up and get mine. I slipped back inside her. "You do feel good."

"Hmmm, so do you baby. Aw shit, you know what, baby, I forgot to tell that I think your toilet is broken."

I grabbed her waist, "Wha…what did you just say?"

"Well, it was making a strange noise, but that can wait, boy. I'm 'bout to work this dick out."

"Oh … hel … Oh hell naw, NAW!" I hopped out of bed and ran to the bathroom. I tried to flush the toilet, but it made a wrenching sound; she killed it! This heifer killed my toilet! I slowly backed away from the bathroom. Pam crept her nasty ass behind me and kissed my shoulders.

"Come on, baby, we'll take care of it later."

I quickly spun around and walked past her, "Get yo nasty, rotgut, cantaloupe-turd droppin' ass out!" I shouted.

"What? I know you just playin'!"

I put on my clothes. "Do I look I'm playin'!
You have thoroughly desecrated my damn bathroom.
Most motherfuckers break a box spring or even a
headboard, a coffee table on occasion, but a fuckin'
toilet?! You done over shitted up my bathroom,
stanked up my apartment damn to all hell, I got little
shit crumbs in the sheets. This is some bullshit!"

"Negro, you got some issues! Something
wrong with you!"

"Me! You the one got this apartment
smelling like damnit I'll bite you!   Something wrong
with your insides! You need a colon cleansing with
some holy water or something!"

Pam threw on her clothes and headed to the
front door. "Fine! This the last time you ever get a
whiff of this!" were her last words.
"Oh, damn!" I slammed the door. "Stanky!" I
screamed after her.

Michael and Kyle are laughing on the floor.
Michael catches his breath and grabs my arm, "So,
you kicked her ass out?"

"Hell, yeah!"

"You couldn't close your eyes and fuck her?"

"Hell, naw!"

"Man, you suppose to be a solider!"

"Dude, I surrender."

"You suppose to slay all beasts."

"My sword is broke!"

CHAPTER TEN

THE MISTRESS

MICHAEL

Michael and Kyle flop down on the couch in the living room holding their stomachs from laughing.

"Man, so what about this tape?" I ask trying to get everyone back in check and off my ass. "She not budging, hiding behind some public has a right to know bullshit. So what ya'll wanna do?"

"Ya'll know what that's really about?" Michael leans forward clasping his hands together.

"What?" I ask.

"Just another chickenhead jealous of a successful brotha. Damn, see yet another reason I stopped dealing with her ass. I hate a woman who can't get behind a man who's about something. The more things change, the more they fuckin' stay the same."

I frown looking over to Kyle, then back to Michael and ask, "What do you mean, 'stopped dealing with her ass?'"

"I mean that's why I stopped dealing with her, stopped going out with her."

"What?" Kyle asks. "You used to date Theresa Gomez?"

"Yeah, back in the day in college, only for a few months. I thought ya'll knew this. It was back in my wanna-a-be porn star days. When I was young, dumb, and full of cum, and anything with tits and an ass would get done." Mike and I stare at Kyle.

"What?" Kyle asks.

I shake my head, "Mike, tell me about Theresa."

"Well, what do you wanna know? I think it was about fifteen years ago. I was in my sophomore year of college. It was the summer break; we had Minorties in American History Class together. She was in the row next to mine … "

Everyday I checked her out. I thought I was gonna flunk out 'cause I couldn't take my eyes off of her. I couldn't believe how fine she was. I had to step to her. So on the second day of class, Theresa walks in and starts talking to some of her girls. I thought

162

about makin' my move, but I did even know where to start.

Five minutes later, the professor walks into the classroom. "Ladies and Gentlemen, today I will be assigning the research project and the groups you all will be working with the diligently to complete. Remember this project will be a fifteen-minute presentation on the roles of minorities played in the economic development of America after the Civil Rights Movement. This project is seventy percent of your grade and will be due in two months. These are the groups: Group One Darryl Jennis, Michelle Brady, Jenna Denson. Group Two, Michael Thompson, Maria Jackson, and Theresa Gomez. Group three … "

Maybe a break! At the end of class I walked over to Theresa and Maria, "Hey, I'm Mike."

"Hey, Mike. I'm Theresa and this is Maria." We shook hands.

"Nice to meet you both. You guys wanna go to Denny's to figure out how we gonna tackle this project?"

Theresa gets her books, "Sure, let's go."

We met up at Denny's and started working on the research project. It was the first of many long nights ahead. We pulled all nighters four, five times a week ...

Kyle snaps his fingers. "You know what? Doesn't Theresa look like that porn star Ava Dennis? Honey, got some juicy titties."

We both stare at Kyle.

I frown, "Go watch T.V. in the other room."

Mike shakes his head, "So we'd been working on this project for the last month everyday and the three of us had a real cool vibe, especially Theresa and I. So I decide to test fate ..."

At Denny's, Maria gathered her books after a couple of hours and said, "All right, ya'll, I'm about to head out. I'll print out the graphs this afternoon, and we'll meet back here at seven?"

"Yeah, that'll be cool." I said.

"A'ight then."

"A'ight girl."

After Maria left, Theresa took a sip of coffee and started gathering her materials. "I guess I'll get ready to go to bed."

"Hey, Theresa hold on. Can I talk to you for a second."

"No problem. Let me go to the little girl's room, and I'll be right back."

Theresa got up and headed toward the bathroom. I looked her up and down, stopping at her butt in her tight stonewash black jeans. She was one of the sexiest women I'd ever met and what made it even more intriguing is that she didn't even know it. She didn't seem concerned about her looks, she didn't even wear make up. She was the Anti-Cover Girl. Damn.

A minute later, Theresa came back to the table and sat down.

"So what's up, Man?"

"Well, I don't know. We been working on this project everyday now, and I got to admit, you cool people."

Theresa smiled taking a sip of coffee. "Thanks, you cool people too."

"I know I might be out of place, but you're fine."

Theresa smiled, blushed, and turned her head away, "Why thank you. You're sweet."

"Well if I'm so sweet, why don't you let me take you to dinner sometime?"

"We have dinner all the time."

"I mean without the mountain of books and Maria."

"What's wrong with Maria?"

"Nothing, I like Maria, I just like you more."

"So you asking me out on a date?"

"I'm tryin' too." I laughed nervously.

"Well, I have to be honest. I don't date other students, especially students that I have research projects due with. Sorry, Mikey. I better get going. I'll see you tomorrow."

I picked up my face, sipped my cup of coffee, and watched her walk out of the door, attracting the attention of a group of men entering the restaurant. I had a feeling she was gonna be a challenge, but the bigger the fight, the better the booty or some shit like that. I was down but not out for count. I gathered my books and thought of plan B.

A week later, the three of us presented the research project in front of the class. Afterwards, I jogged up to Theresa in the exit doorway.

"Hey, Theresa."

"Hey, Man. An A, that is cool. My G.P.A. is gonna be on point!"

"Let's celebrate!"

"Okay, I'll let Maria know. Denny's?"

"Well, I was thinking Denny's then a movie for you and me."

"Ah, sounds like a date. That's a no-no."

"No, you said you don't date students that you have research projects due with. Well the project is over, and since we are at the end of the semester, we are technically not students. So how about a movie between friends? I mean unless you gotta a man or something?"

"No, I ain't gotta a man."

"Well what's one movie between friends? We won't even call it a date. You can pay."

Theresa smiles, "Well … "

"Come on…*Attack of the Fifty Foot Platypus* is playing at the Cineplex 38."

Theresa laughed and turned her head away, "A'ight, one movie as friends."

"Cool. I'll call you later."

We went the movie and had a good time. We went out for lunch the next day, had an even better time. We hung out for the next three weeks; it was great time every time. So we're in week four of this fuddy buddy shit. I decide I wanna make something happen tonight. So went go to the show … again and we're walking out from the theater to my car. I wrapped my arm around Theresa's shoulder and leaned in for a kiss. Theresa played it off and turned her cheek. So, I checked my breath and leaned in again. Theresa backs away.

"What's up? I like you, I know you like me, so why the cold shoulder? We've been hanging out a lot the last month. I mean I'd like to be more to you than just a movie buddy ... "

"Well I had a feeling, this was going to come up. I've been thinking about it too, but ... "

"But what? What the problem is?"

"Well, there's a door that only my most intimate friends can walk through. I like you, I do but I ... I ... "

I stepped closer to Theresa, gently placing my hands on her arms. She pushed my arms back.

"You can tell me, what you don't worship the devil or nothing?"

Theresa shyly looked away, "Naw. Nothing like that."

"Then?"

Theresa paused and rolled her eyes, "I can't believe I'm telling you this ... "

"You got me nervous ... " I said.

Theresa sighed. "I'm a dominatrix."

"So ... "

"I have been trained to give pleasure through the voluntary submission and ultimate dominance of my lovers."

"So what you like to be in charge? That's cool with me."

"It's more complex than that."

"Look, I have a pretty open mind. So, if you want take charge from time to time and get a little rough, I'm a big boy."

"It's more than that, it's more of a spiritual commitment, a relationship, an agreement. It's kind a hard to explain."

"Look, I'm not looking to play you or nothin'. I want something real. I'm cool with a working towards a commitment. Why don't we just take this slowly to another level and see what happens?"

"I guess that makes sense. I do like you … I'll think about it, fair?"

"Cool," I said, feeling pretty good about the future.

The school year began without a word from Theresa. One night, I got off work and went home to begin studying for a Chemistry test. It was about 8:00, and I was in the kitchen studying when suddenly the phone rings. I grabbed a glass of milk and answered it.

"Hello"

"Hey, it's me. Are you busy?"

"Hey Theresa, girl, what's up? Where you been all this time? I haven't heard from you in weeks."

"Inside myself thinking, a lot about you actually."

"Really, well I'm honored." I sat down at the table.

"You should be. I've thought about it and if you are ready to come through the door, I'm ready to guide you through my walls."

"Really! The hell you say!" I dropped the glass of milk.

"I hope you're ready for me. Be here, it's apartment 1296 B, at ten o' clock sharp!"

"Ten o' clo ... " I said as Theresa abruptly hangs up the phone.

I hung up the phone. "Ready? Shit, I'm bout to tear the kitty up!"

I ran to the bathroom, showered, put on my best smelling aftershave, and raced over to Theresa's place to be there at ten. I wanted this coochie so bad I could taste it. I sprinted up twelve flights of stairs to

Theresa's apartment. I was out of breath looking around for apartment 1296 B. The elevator dinged behind me. I was so focused on the draws that my dumb ass didn't even know there was an elevator. Some kat steps out the elevator,

"Excuse me … Bro … you … you know where 1296 B is?" I asked breathless.

"Yeah, Man. It's down the hallway and last place on the right," he said, snickering. He shook his head and went into his apartment. I brushed it off and ran down to her place.

I didn't know I was outta shape or just in shape for some. This had to be the longest fuckin' hallway in the world. I finally got there, wiped off the sweat, and knocked on the door. I stood there dick hard, straightening out my clothes. She answered the door wearing a skin tight, jet black latex outfit.

I looked her over. Shit, you could see everything. Damn she must have poured a bucket of latex all over her naked body. Baby had more nooks and crannies than a freakin' English muffin.

"Come in and sit down."

I sat down on the couch in the living room. It was kinda dark, but I could clearly see the high heel thigh high black leather boots she was sportin'. She bent over, rubbed her hands across her coffee table, and grabbed a black horsewhip. She rubbed the whip across her body like it was a natural part of her as she walked over to the couch. She raised one of her legs on the couch and pushed the whip handle into my shoulder. I sat down on the couch.

"No, on the floor with your leg's crossed." I complied. Shoot, I was ready to bend over and lick my own ass if it meant I was gonna get some of this.

Theresa sat in a huge throne-like chair across the room. "Good, you take directions well. Here are the rules: you will do as I say, exactly as I say to the letter. In this relationship, I am your master and you are my dog. Now be a good dog and put this on."

Theresa threw me a dog collar. I knew this was gonna be hot! I quickly put it on, "Oh, I can play along."

"Quiet!" Theresa cracked her whip, piercing my ears. "My dogs do not speak unless I say, and when that time comes, you address me as Mistress Theresa."

Theresa placed her foot into my chest and pushed me to the ground. "You lack discipline, Dog, and I'm afraid you will have to be housebroken. When I snap my fingers, you will lick my boots clean. You will not stop until I snap my fingers again. If you do a good job … "

Theresa rubbed her hands over her breasts.

" … you get a reward. If you don't … " Theresa smacked the floor with her whip, "you will be punished."

Theresa snapped her fingers as she placed her mud-covered boots on my shoulder. I really wanted this pussy so I grabbed them and began to lick away. In the meantime, she picks up the phone and starts talking to one of her girls.

After a while my tongue is feelin' like sandpaper, but all I can think about suckin' on those big ass titties. I'm licking the top, sides, bottom of the boots, getting fuckin' tongue cramp, and she's on the phone not even skippin a beat. I'm singing in my head…'I'm gonna suck some titties, I'm gonna suck some titties.'

Eventually I look at the clock on the wall its one o' clock which means I've licked these damn boots for almost two and a half hours!

Theresa hung up the phone and snapped her fingers. I sat up like a faithful dog with a sore tongue and throbbing dick about to receive a big reward. She blew me a kiss and bounced a meaty bone dog treat off the top of my head.

"Good boy. You're dismissed." Theresa walked into the bedroom and locked the door.

I stare at the door with a muddy face and pout for about twenty minutes. I know she coming back out here. She never did. I got a mouthful of mud and that's all I get?

For two weeks, every night, we did this! I'm thinking every night I'm about to get some trim and wind up licking these dirty ass boots for two hours.

"Are you serious?" Kyle asked.

"Kyle, I couldn't make this shit up. Every day she must have been stompin' in mud somewhere. Every time I went over, her boots were dirtier than the night before. So for the fifthteenth night I'm at Theresa's place on my knees … "

Theresa paced in front of me all I could focus on was her dirty ass boots. She smacked her whip and said, "I like you, Dog. Today you have earned a big treat. Something soft, tight, and wet would you like that?"

"Yes Mistress Theresa!" About freakin' time, I reached around in my back pocket to get a rubber.

"Turn around and strip."

Aw shit, it's on, it's on! I turned around and got undressed. I was ready to tear it up!!! I turned back around and Theresa handed me a pair of black leather chaps, black leather underwear with the words 'stankin' bitch' embroiled in fuckin diamond studs, and a red child-size cowboy hat.

"Put this on."

"What?"

"What?" Theresa cracked the bullwhip, lashing out a candle flame behind me. "I don't negotiate with dogs, and I don't like repeating myself! Put it on! You are now promoted from Dog to Bitch."

This is a lot to put on for some sex, but shoot I didn't care, I was just thinking about that wet soft reward I was suppose to be getting. Theresa removed the dog collar and put and a leather leash around my throat. Aw…this gonna be some freaky year 2012 shit.

"I promised you something soft, smooth, and tight." Theresa grabs the leash and yanks me to the bathroom and hands me a soapy sponge. "Here's something soft and wet. Clean my house, you Stankin' Bitch, and thank your master for your reward. You have one hour."

I lowered my head, "Thank you, Mistress." and started to wipe down the bathtub...

"Hold on a second! Tell me ... dawg ... playa ... tell me did not let this chick call you a Stankin' Bitch and you thank her and clean her house," I say as Kyle and I stare with draped open mouths.

"Yeah, Man, I did."

"Oh, hell, naw!" Kyle and I scream, laughing on the floor.

Michael shakes his head, hiding his face.

"Tell me ... tell me ... tell me you at least hit it at that point. Tell me you got it."

"Man, there's more ... "

I washed the dishes in the sink pulling this little ass underwear out of my butt. Suddenly an alarm clock bell rang. I jumped up startled. I bent down to clean up the spilled water on the floor.

"What the hell?" I looked around to see where the alarm was coming from.

"Time's up! Bring yo stankin' ass here!" Theresa screamed from the living room and yanks the leash around my throat. I slipped on the water on the kitchen floor and next thing I know I'm being dragged along the floor. My head crashed in the doorway as I crawl to the living room. Then she yanked me along the house as she checked my work.

"You done well, Bitch. Go home," she said ,dropping the leash.

Theresa left and shut her door. There I was again, on the floor looking around. "Where's my clothes?"

"What is with you and fuckin' dressin up!" Kyle asks slamming his fist on the coffee table. "I can't believe this shit."

"Man, I'm still thinking about the nappy. So again we doing this shit for three weeks and finally, finally … "

One night I was standing outside Theresa's door, in a long overcoat. Theresa opens the door looking pissed. "You're late!" she snapped.

"I'm sorry Mistress. I had a midterm and… "

Theresa cracked her whip an inch away my ear. I cringed. "One, did I ask you to speak? Two, do you think I want some bullshit-ass excuse?"

"No, Mistress."

"Don't waste my time again. On your knees, Bitch. Today I have an important job for you. Your Mistress is lonely tonight; pleasure me with your mouth until I say stop and if you come up for air without me cumming, you will be severely punished. Now!"

Theresa whipped back the long leather coat concealing her neatly shaved womanhood. I dropped to my knees and placed my head in her lap. Theresa moaned.

An hour passed, and Theresa stood up and rubbed her fingers through her hair, "Ummm, you've done well, Bitch. You have earned a promotion to slave. Disrobe and please me. Now!"

I picked her up and placed her against the closest wall. Weeks of frustrating humiliation had come to the surface as I took her ...

Kyle claps his hands, "So, you finally got some. Finally!"

"Yeah Man, but that's when the shit really got twisted. I'm having freaky circus sex with this girl. I'm hitting it like a champion, and I'm thinking finally I got my nuts back, I'm gonna show this girl who the real Mandingo is. I'm hittin' it like a billion dollar gigolo. Then … "

Theresa pushed me away from her. She smiled flirtatiously. I smiled back, looking her over. She pulled me down for a slow wet kiss and then she pushed me up and slapped me in the face! She hit me so hard I fell about ten feet from the coochie and rolled in the damn kitchen! My mouth was throbbin'!

"What the fuck!"

"Ah, my little slave has a pair of balls after all. Good, let me sit on them."

She threw me down on the floor and straddled me, "I hope you don't mind I get a little wild sometimes."

I rubbed her back while she kissed my neck. "No damn, just take it easy." I said rubbing my jaw.

"Let me make it up to you Baby, how versed are you in autoerotism?"

"I've been around the block a few times."

"You ever scarfed?"

"Sure … sure … I've scarfed a lot."

"Well, I guess I can take you to a new level."

"Oh yeah, take me to heaven Ba … "

Before I could finish my sentence, Theresa yanked the leash around my throat. I gagged for air as she wrapped the slack around her arm and continued to ride me, moaning as pulled the leash hard.

This bitch was trying to kill me. I'm straining to talk, "I … I can't bre … I … I can't bre … breath … Stop … Stop!!!"

She dropped the leash, I coughed as my eyes welled up with tears. I pulled the leash off as she looked down on me smiling.

I rubbed my throat, "Have you lost your fuckin' mind?" I asked … .

"So you let her whoop yo ass?" Kyle asks.

"Man I didn't know anything about that autoertica crap. I thought that meant we were gonna fuck in the car! Shit I was about to grab my hat!"

"So what happened next?" Kyle asks.

"You ain't gonna believe this, but I still wanted to hit it. I was just tryin' to get my nut off …

I figured, I'm about to show this gal the Man in me, how the Thompsons get down! So I flipped her over on her back, dug my toes into the carpet, wrapped her legs around my waist, and started drilling. I was gonna make this chick say my name. First, I did the slow groove, then the Kansas City Crunk. Then I went old school with the New Jack gutterslut swing, and then oh … oh then I unleashed the force! I'm sweatin' like a pervert at prom, and the chick ain't battin' an eye. She might as well been eatin' a steak."

"Harder! Harder! Put your back into it! Come on! Please your Mistress!" She screamed diggin' her nails in my ass.

I pumped hard, about to climax, "Oh God! Oh God! ARRGGGHH!"
My body tingled, as I closed my eyes and succumbed to rapture collapsing on her.

Five minutes pass and I looked down at Theresa looking disappointed like a kid who got passed over by Santa. "I know you are not done," she groaned.

I smiled and put my head back on those huge titties, "Yeah that was good."

"I gather." She rolled her eyes.

I raised my head, "Girl you just got some good stuff. Just let me recharge and … "

"You stankin' bitch!" was the last thing I heard as she punched me in the jaw.

I woke up the next morning, rubbin' my throbbing head. I looked around at the pieces of the coffee table I guess I fell into. I got up, put on my overcoat, and saw Theresa in the kitchen making breakfast like nothing happened. My head was bumpin' like I had just fought a damn man. I just got knocked the fuck out and she makin' waffles and grits. It was like a bad dream.

She walked over to me, yeah I cringed a little bit, but she reached in to give me a kiss, "Hey, Sweetie. Sit down, you want some juice?"

I sat down, looking at Theresa like she just fell out the Twilight Zone. She poured me a glass of orange juice. The doorbell rang, even that made my head hurt. Theresa left to the get the door as I put the glass of juice against my head.

Theresa came back into the kitchen. "Hey, Baby, you gonna be ready to go in fifteen? Maria's in the other room."

"Go? Where we going?"

"Six Flags, silly, don't you remember?"

"Oh yeah. Yeah give me a few."

"Great, I laid your clothes out. I want my Man looking good with me."

"Ya'll are so cute. Where is the sink so I can throw up?" Maria says getting a glass of orange juice.

I put my clothes on and headed out to Maria's car, a tiny two-door tugboat on wheels. I'm 6'4 and they about 5'3 so I get in the front seat to stretch out.

"You like my new ride? It's so cute but it's a little tight, let me put the seat back."

Theresa put on her sunglasses. "No, it's okay I can get in the front, and Mike can stretch out in the back."

I look in the nonexistent backseat and think to myself. "In the back? What am I suppose to do sit in the trunk, hang my legs out the window of this shiny ass dick on wheels."

Theresa patted me on the back and said, "Just lay back in the backseat and relax."

"Just lay back and relax? I might as well go to Six Flags in a damn suitcase."

Theresa smiled. "Oh, Babe, you're funny. Come on get in the back so we can go." She kissed my cheek and wrapped her arms around my right arm.

"We can take your car if you want to Mike. I'll kick in for gas." Maria said.

"That'll work. I got the gas don't worry, " I said pullin' out my keys.

"No, don't be silly, your car will be fine. Besides you already filled the tank. This will be fine, right Baby?" Theresa grinned.

"Well, I can reimburse you for the gas," I said pulling out my wallet.

Theresa pulled me down and leaned in to whisper in my ear, "Get your stankin' ass in the back before I whoop your bitch ass again."

Shocked, I looked at her. She was stoned faced serious!

So, I get in the back, "Well, it looks kinda cozy back here." I sat with my knees to my chest in the back while Maria and Theresa danced to house music in the front ...

In the kitchen, Kyle and I sit frozen, just looking at Michael. I had to say something. "Man, you a punk Dude. I can see how Debra got you in some damn pink ass panties, Man. I can't take no more of this shit. How long this go on?"

"We must have messed around for a couple of months, it just got to the point that she was trying to be the man of the relationship. We go to the restaurant she ordering for me, we go to the movie she holdin' me, putting her arm around me like I'm the chick, when it got to the point when I'm serving her and her girls sandwiches during the NFL Playoffs I had to be out."

I can't believe this stuff, "Let me get this straight. She put you in leather panties with diamond sequins on them, she punked your ass in the car, she popped you to the eye for cumming too fast, she almost choked yo dumb ass out, twice, dragged you around her house like a freakin' mutt, and servin' some damn sandwiches was your call to glory? That was the day you had to get your nuts back?"

"Truth be told X, her stuff was good, Man."
"You have truly fucked yourself retarded."
"It wasn't just the punany, it was the fact that she knew what she was doin.' Baby was a freak, video, toys, she was down for anything. She made

this video for me for my birthday of us screwing on this real nice oak kitchen table. It was kinda like the one you got at your place. That shit was hot."

My cell phone rings. "And all you had to do was take a punch in the eye. Don't tell nobody else this shit. I'm gonna get back at you on that later."

I answer my phone. "Hello. Hey, Gina, what's up?"

"Hey X, I was hoping to get you," Gina says over the cell phone. "How are you?"

"I'm all right. How you doing?"

"I don't know. Are you mad at me?"

"Naw, just takin' it all in. Look, I'm at my brother's house, and we're about to head out. Let me call you back."

"Please call, okay? I've been thinking about you."

"A'ight, I'll call you later." I hang up the phone.

Michael puts on a jacket, "Was that Gina?"

"Yeah, Man."

"Yeah, yesterday was supposed to be the big day! What's up?"

"Oh, Man, I got so wrapped up in your shit, I forgot to fill ya'll in on this. Aw, damn. Come on. I got an idea on how we gonna get you out of this shit."

      We leave the house and drive off in my truck.

      "So where we going Man?" Michael asks as he puts on his seat belt.

      "I'm droppin' ya'll off at Headquarters, and I'm going to do a little research for a story of my own."

CHAPTER ELEVEN

DOGGIE STYLE

XAVIER

I merge into traffic on my way to Michael's Campaign Headquarters. I wish I could focus on the mission at hand, but hearing Gina's voice sent my mind in a thousand different directions.

"So what's up with this plan X?" Michael asks.

"I ain't got it all worked out yet, but trust me the wheels are turning."

"And what's up with this Gina anyway?" Kyle asks.

"You remember that I met Gina at the gym during my Capoeira class?" I tell him.

"Capoeira?"

"It's this African-Brazilian art form, Kyle. It's the fighting method that slaves used in Brazil to fight against their oppressors."

"That's the one that is kinda a dance too?" Michael asks.

"Right. It mixes martial arts with dance. Anyway, I'm in class and I see this fine caramel honey walking to the Stairmaster and, man, my head was on a swivel! She was about 5'9-5'10, full figured, shaped just right, and working every inch of it. Plus she was sportin' those kinda retro black librarian type glasses."

Kyle giggles. "Aw, yeah I like that."

"You know she had me. But this one, there was something about her. I had to step to it. So, I went back to playing Capoeira with the group."

"I'm surprised you even went back to class." Michael says and smiles big time.

"Man, I almost got my head knocked off. At any rate the class ended, and I got ready to make my move. I jumped on the treadmill behind her and damn that booty bouncing up and down had me tripping. I swear it was like a symphony or something."

My heart was pumpin' hard as I made my through the line of treadmills. Her brown shoulder length hair covered in sweat was sexy, almost primal. I'd seen a couple of gold tooth wearin' kats trying to step to her with that O. G. playa rap. She didn't seem interested. I hopped on the empty treadmill next to her and tried to the play the dumb role fumbling around on the machine. I knew it wasn't the tightest rap, but I had to try something to get in the door.

I tapped Gina on the arm, "Excuse me. Hi, do you know how to turn on the computer on this thing."

Gina looked me over, "Sure, just press this button that says 'Computer On'."

"Ah, thanks." I chuckled. "By the way, I'm Xavier. I know I'm being forward but I had to come over a meet you. You are breathtaking. I couldn't even focus in class when you came in. Would you like to maybe get something to eat after your workout?"

Gina smiled, "Thanks but, I … "

"I understand, I was a little forward. Honestly, I just saw a dime and got carried away. Can I give you my card?"

"Look Brotha, I gotta be honest with you, I just got out of a situation, and I'm not looking to meet anybody. I just came in for the workout."

"I can respect that. Maybe we can workout together sometime?"

"Maybe, we'll see."

"Maybe is cool. Maybe is definitely cool. Well, I'll let you get back to your workout. I didn't get your name."

"I'm Gina."

"I would shake your hand, but you ain't tryin' to meet nobody. I'll just nod as say 'what's up' the next time I see you, cool?"

"You're silly, Boy. Sure, I'll see you."

"All right pleasure not to meet you Gina."

Gina shyly giggled, "Pleasure not to meet you to Xavier."

I made her laugh, at least that's something …

Every Thursday for the next few weeks, I saw her. I figured I'd run with the little crack in the ice I made. So, I played it cool. I knew if I was going to get in, I was going to have to chill and wait for the right time. For the next few weeks, I just nodded or smiled when I saw her until one night, opportunity knocked. She was heading out to her car, and I noticed she looked like she was a little sore. She was limping to her car, dragging her gym bag behind her.

"Gina? Hey Gina !"

Gina stopped to rub her calf as I ran up to her, "Hey, are you okay?"

"Yeah, I just overdid it a little."

"Yeah, I saw you working it out on the treadmill. Started feeling good. You put that bastard on Level 10, huh?"

Gina laughed. "Yeah, I was cool for about twenty seconds."

"I bet, thought you were running the Chicago Marathon."

"Yeah, you didn't see me fall off the treadmill, did you?"

"And crash into the wall? Then roll down the stairs into the snack shop? Yep."

Gina laughed and covered her face with her hands. "Dang, you saw that? Oh God, I thought I was by myself."

"I was just coming out to the shower room, and I saw you doing the baseball slide down the stairs, looking like you goin' into home plate."

Gina laughed hard, covering her face again, "Damn, I'm so embarrassed!"

I laughed, feeling a little more cocky. "It's all right, we've all been there. Let me get your bag."

"Thanks my car is right over there."

We walked through the garage for a minute, two minutes, five, ten …

"Damn, I can't believe this. I lost my car. I hate when I do this crap. Look I hate to have you just wandering the garage with me. Why don't you just give me my bag, and I'll find it. Besides my leg is killin' me." She said squatting down to massage her calf. I figured I try something a little bold, so I swooped down and picked her up.

"WHAT THE HELL YOU DOING, BOY!" she cried out.

"Relax, my truck is on the next floor. Let me carry you to the elevator, we'll head up there, and I'll drive you around."

"Well, I don't know, I don't … "

"I tell you what, here are the keys. You drive my truck, and I'll sit in the passenger's seat."

"All right, all right. I guess I can trust you but don't try anything funny. To the elevator!" She smiled, pointing the way as I carried her to the elevator and then to my truck. It took about ten minutes, but we found her car.

"I feel so stupid. I'm sorry to put you through this," she said as she pulled next to the car.

"Girl, it ain't no thang. You know how many times I've done this? Shoot this is my fourth truck this year. I just give up after a hour."

She laughed as I went over to the driver's side and gently helped her out the truck. I think she liked the attention 'cause she wasn't putting up nearly as much of a fight. I just hope she wasn't getting used to this shit cause baby girl was getting heavy.

"Thank you so much. I feel so embarrassed. You didn't have to do all of this."

"I told you it is not a problem. You make sure you take care of that leg."

"Yeah, I'll probably take it easy for a week or two, but when I come back, maybe we can work out together."

"Oh, so does this mean we've met?"

"Yeah, I guess so. Since you helped me to my car, I guess I can introduce myself. I'm Gina Walterson."

"Xavier Thompson."

"It' s a pleasure to meet you, Xavier Thompson."

"Same here. You're so secretive I thought you were a ninja or something."

"You're so silly." She giggled. She was cute, but she had a laugh like a hyena at an orgy.

"Naw, I'm just playin'. Well, I'll let you get home. I hope to see you at the gym soon."

"When I come back, I'll definitely save a treadmill for you," she said.

"Cool. You just make sure it's one a couple spaces down, just in case you decide to missile yourself out a window or something."

"See you got jokes, a'ight, a'ight."

"You know I'm kiddin.' Hopefully I'll see you soon, Gina."

"See ya, Xavier."

Gina started the engine and drove off. I headed back to my truck, feeling a small victory had been won.

Kyle rolls the toothpick in his mouth around. "See, that's your problem, Big Bro. You play the saint roll too much. Tryin' to be Billy Dee, carrying this random chick around like a broke off horse. I gotta school you on how to mack."

"Why don't you mack your ass back there and get my sunglasses, Astroglide!"

"Aw, why you bringin' up old shit?"

I pull up behind Michael's Campaign Headquarters.

"Back to Gina. After the night at the garage, we started working out every Thursday and then we hangin' out a little bit more and a little more and a little more. So, we were getting along, and the booty is looking better and better each week. I figure I gotta make my move. I asked her to go out dancing, she said yes, and we hit the town. First date cool, second date even better, third date even better than that. Now normally you know the rule, three dates something gotta happen, but I wanted to play it cool so I figured I give it a little more time. You know, let this thick Georgia Peach ripen."

"A'ight I feel you, I feel you," Michael says.

"Now don't laugh, but for the next six months … "

"Six months! You ain't hit in six months?" Kyle says, droppin' his toothpick.

"I know, I know, but I like this chick. All during this time, we doing the *When Harry Met Sally* routine, just hangin out, getting to know each other, shit like that."

Kyle scoots up. "Six months! You slippin,' dawg, you slippin.'"

"I know yo' greasy ass ain't talking about slippin.' I got Fred's number on speed dial Negro, watch yo'self. Anyway, I'm telling ya'll this girl has it. She is fine, plus she was cool to hang with."

"Well, ya'll doing some heavy makin' out or something right?"

"Naw, Kyle, not even that. Not even a kiss."

"Mike, you hearin' this shit."

"I know, lil' bro. I can't believe it either."

"Can I finish? I really liked her, so I wanted to play it right. I thought she was maybe an old fashioned girl; wanted to save herself for marriage, but I could tell by the way she walked and carried herself that she wasn't that innocent."

Kyle rolls his eyes and says, "Wake me up when this shit is over!"

"Anyway, we doing all this hangin' out, but we ain't getting physical. I ain't saying I gotta hit it, but damn, no kiss, no making out, no dry humping, nothing. So I have to ask her, shit, we ain't 13 years old, what's up?

It was a Sunday morning in July. I called Gina at eight a.m. to invite her to have brunch in the park near the Downtown Canal. She sounded really excited to meet, and since she didn't have any objections to meeting on Sunday morning I figured she wasn't super religious. It had to be some other reason that she didn't wanna get down. I had a little French theme goin' since she always talked about going to Paris one day. I bought some croissants, homemade strawberry preserves, thin sliced honey baked spiral ham from the corner deli, some red grapes, little French style strawberry cheese cake torts, and some iced French Vanilla Cappuccino. As always we were having a good time, just talking, looking out at the gondola boats gliding slowly across the Canal. We packed up brunch and walked along the pink tulip petal covered Canal sidewalks holding hands. The blue water sparkled alongside the walkways as a group children brushed by us. She looked on and smiled. "You like kids, Xavier?"

"I don't know. Kids are like White Castles, you gotta in the mood for them and they can't stay too long. They gotta get in and get out."

"So you don't wanna have any?"

"I ain't sayin' that. With the right woman, a couple of shorties would be cool. But you can't raise kids like you used to be able to. You can't beat 'em. I telling you if whuppin' a kid's ass was an Olympic sport, my mama would be a gold medalist. I can just see her now on the winner's podium with a tree switch in one hand, a extension cord   strapped to her hip, and a gun belt with a rolling pin in one on holster and a wooden spoon she called 'Charlie" in the other. You can't do kids like that anymore. Now we have time out, which is some crap. All it's doing is givin' them a breather to do some more bad shit in a minute. I believe in ghetto, military time out."

"So, what you gonna do, have the kids doing push ups and stuff."

"Naw, I'm gonna make punishment a sport. I'm gonna hook up the electricity up to a treadmill. Ya'll lil' bad asses wanna play Playstation, get to running. Even the baby, you wanna watch Barney, you better pedal your little butt off on your big wheel."

"Boy, you silly."

"What about you, you want kids?"

"Yeah, I'd like a little girl or even a knot-headed little boy someday. If the right man came along."

"And what kind of man would that be?"

"Well, I don't know, someone with Denzel's charm, Michael Jordan's smile, Steve Harvey's sense of humor and style, and Morris Chestnut's body. But they gotta be a Godly man like Kirk Franklin with thug 2-Pac twist."

"Damn, girl, that's a hell of mix. What you want a Black Frankenstein?"

"Naw, seriously I want what every woman wants just a good strong, real man."

"Hmmm, I guess that makes sense."

"And you?"

"I want what everyman wants, a lady in the streets but a freak in the sheets."

"Of course, men!" Smiling, she turned her head.

"Really I just want a good woman. Somebody that is gonna have my back and, will put my back out from time to time."

"You got a little freak in ya, don't ya?" she asked.

"Well, why don't you be the judge?"

I gently grabbed Gina's waist and spun her around to me. "They say you can tell a lot about a person by their kiss."

I gently grasped her cheek and slowly drew her in. She closed her eyes and moved closer. Then suddenly she stopped...

"What? What's wrong?" I asked.

Gina grabbed my upper arms to hold herself back, "Look, I like you, I just want to take things slow. When the time is right, one day I'll make it up to you. Just be patient, you won't regret it."

Michael stared stoned faced at me. "Damn what was her problem? I mean I can respect takin' things a little slow, but six months? Come on, what's up?"

"Well, hey. At any rate, so there I am waiting again, two more months, my nuts so full they draggin' on the floor. Almost nine months without some, and I'm not seeing anyone else, still trying to get with her. You all know how I am when I don't get any."

"A fucking bitch!" Kyle and Michael say simultaneously.

"Right, and that night, I went to Capoeria class mad and horny…"

In the workout center in Capoeria class, we were gathered around in a circle. Some of the students were playing music, while others were clapping to the beat. Jimmy and Michelle jumped in the middle of the circle and started simulating a fight by throwing some fierce kicks. I was clapping off beat and pissed off. My face was balled up in a knot.

Eventually it is my turn to play in the middle of the circle. I stomped in, fuck the beat!

Jimmy was in the circle, dancing back and forth, taunting me. Now, what was suppose to happen was that we were suppose just to mix in and throw kicks, takedowns, and fakes. Along with our dance steps, we try to trick each other into falling on the ground or out of the circle without touching. But ah, naw, not that. I scrunched my face up and snarled like a hungry lion. I knew it was about be some shit, because Jimmy's eyes moved to the left then right. "What's wrong with you?" he asked hesitantly.

"Come on, bitch," I growled tackling his ass. He acted like a punk, scratching up the floor with his fingernails and trying to get away. The group separated us, and I stormed out the gym. I gotta apologize to Jim too, that was real foul.

Well the next morning at 6:00 A.M. the phone rang in my apartment. I fumbled around out of my sleep to reach for the phone on the dresser.
"Hello."
"Xavier, Man what's up. This is Benny."

I wiped my eyes and grabbed the clock, "Hey man what's crackin'?"

"What you got going on today? You wanna make a couple of bucks?"

"I'm on vacation. What's happening?"

"One of my guys called off, everyone else is off sick or on vacation, and I've been on for twenty-one days straight. I don't have a bailiff for Courtroom A Downtown. I know it's been a while, but you're trained. If you want the shift, it's yours for double time. You'd be doing me a big favor."

"Yeah man, that's cool. Who's the judge?"

Benny shuffled paper over the phone. "Uh, Lopez."

"A'ight, she's cool. Nine?"

"Yeah Nine A.M."

"Cool, I'll be there."

"A'ight and thanks, dawg."

"You know you owe me, Benny, right?"

"As long as I owe you, you'll never be broke. Peace."

I hung up the phone, reset the alarm, and went back to sleep. Later that day, courtroom proceedings were going on, and I was standing in the corner of the room, watching over everything. In retrospect, I know I picked the wrong damn day to do this shit. It seems like every fine ass chick in Indy caught a case today. I was drooling at the honeys, all perfect ten's coming in and out of the courtroom. The plaintiffs, defendants, witnesses…FINE! The courtroom reporter…FINE! The damn judge…FINE! By the fourth case of the day, I'm squirmin' in the corner, sweatin' with angry blue balls.   Lunch break begins. I'm ready to pounce on anything in skirt. I followed around a chick that looked like Grady from *Sanford and Son* for twenty minutes. She was about seventy, at least, but she had ass so I was down.

Shit now, I know what Kyle feels like. An hour later, the afternoon session began, and I'm back in the front of the courtroom, sweatin'.

"All rise!" I called out as Judge Lopez makes her way out. I guess some of the people didn't hear me; they still talking and sittin' they asses down. So I slam my fist on the bench and in a louder voice say, "Get up! Up! The honorable Judge Lopez has entered the courtroom! Get UP!"

Judge Lopez approached the bench, lookin' at me funny.

"Sit down!" I bark.

Judge Lopez whispered, "You okay, Xavier?"

"I'm fine, Your Honor."

"Are you sure?"

"Yes. I'm sure."

She stared at me. "All right then, call the first case."

In the truck, Kyle shakes his head in pity, "Damn, damn, damn, Dude, this chick has got you twisted. I would have just jacked off in the bathroom."

"Naw, man I'm hungry. That would be like given a man who ain't ate for a week a soda cracker. I needed a full plate and then some. I'm bout ready to step to anyone, she could have been 410 pounds with a stank gold tooth, a Jerri Curl weave, termite infested wooden leg, and I wouldn't have give a damn! I had to get some. I had to!"

Anyway, I'm mad the whole afternoon. I'm slamming down the files on my desk, swearin' people, in pissed off, snatchin' papers from the parties. I'm in the corner, givin' witnesses the stink eye to hurry up. I even tore one of the damn doors to the chambers off the hinge. I'm a mess. So the day ends, and I get into my truck, back up, floored it, and peeled out of the parking lot. I launched the truck off the ramp airborne about what had to be fifty feet onto the street. I'm about to go to my black book before my nuts get stuck in a door or something!

Just then the cell phone rings, "Gotdamnit, what!"

Gina answered, "Xavier! You okay?"

"Yeah, yeah just rough day."

"Why don't we get together and see if we can make it a better night."

"What are you talking about? I can't go for no more walks on the Canal right now."

"I thought about what you said, and if you still mean it, come over in an hour."

"For what Bid Whiz, Scrabble, Checkers … "

"No, but I might let you get a jump in so you can king me."

"What you talking about?" I wanted to make sure there wasn't any trickery afoot.

"Look, come over and bring me something hard, Black, and thick for me to sit on. Is that clear enough, or you want me to run out in the street butt naked?"

"For real? You sure?"

"Definitely and bring an overnight bag. It's gonna be a long, *hard* night."

Shit, I slammed on the brakes and spun the steering wheel on the truck around. I had that bitch on two wheels! I sped in the opposite direction, ran home, crashed face first in the front door tryin' to get the key in. I threw whatever clean clothes I could find into my overnight bag. I ran down the hallway, clothes hanging out of the bag back to my truck. I started the engine and sped to Gina's house. I sprinted up the stairs, my tie is on sideways. I knocked on the door, like I was the police. I was about ready to break this chick's door in half. I was pacing in front of door when Gina came out in the tight red dress and matching Stilettos.

"Do you like?" Gina twirled around. I couldn't say nothin.' I damn near came right then and there. "I thought you would. Why don't you come on in?"

I shook off the daze and thought, "Fin-al-fuck-in-ly," as I dropped the suitcase on the living room floor. The interior of the home was clean and very frilly, like a little girl's bedroom that grew like a weed and took over the rest of the house. Everything from top to bottom is covered in the same shade of pink. It was like being trapped inside a giant strawberry Twinkie. There were dozens of stuffed animals, all pink and mostly dogs, all over the couch. I panned the rooms and stopped at the back wall and looked at dozens pictures and paintings of dogs. I looked down as a little terrier brushed by one the two ceramic dogs near the doorway of the kitchen.

"Wow, you like dogs, huh?"

"How can you tell?"

"Just a guess."

Gina picked up the terrier. "Yeah, I love dogs. Pete, here is the kindest and most loyal little thing in the world. What about you? Do you like dogs?"

"Yeah, they're cool."

"Good, because all my special friends have to like my little doggie … ," Gina leaned into my ear and whispered, "… before they can pet my little kitty." I could have fucked her right there in front of Pete's little ass. I played it cool.

"Oh, really," I drooled.

"Put your tongue back in your mouth. Dinner's almost ready. Come on in the kitchen."

Gina put the dog down and led me into the kitchen. I stared her up and down, wondering how she possibility got into this skin-tight dress. She tugged it down over her thighs and pulled out a seat for me. I loved this moment, the time before you know you are about to get some. I love the anticipation, the build up of imagining all the positions, all the sounds, smells and tastes of the night ahead. I lived for this!

I looked around the kitchen, savoring the moment. The kitchen was a little more normal than the living room. She had candlelight, jazz on the stereo, and a bottle of wine chillin' on table.

"Dinner smells great," I complimented.

"Yeah, it's my specialty; a little Chi-town favorite." Gina put the plates on the table and sat down.

"Hot dogs?"

"Yep, Chicago style. Dig in." Gina turned around to get to get some glasses chilling in the fridge. A little weird, but maybe this is all she knows how to cook. Shit, I didn't care; I didn't wanna eat anyway. She poured two glasses of wine, and we ate dinner.

"These are good."

"You really like them?"

"Yeah they're good, a little different but really good. Almost as good as the ones on Maxwell Street in Chicago."

"Good, eat up there's plenty. You're going to need your strength."

"For what? Are we playing Frizzbee later?"

"Naw, but we might do a little puppy play later."

"Oh … ho … ho, really?" I laughed.

"Oh, definitely. By the way, I plan on checking out some art this weekend at the Starving Artist's Expo. After your brother's speech, will you have time to maybe check out some of the booths with me?"

"Yeah, we can check out some art. Get a little something to eat at the Café Boatyard and get out the to Music Celebration."

"Sounds like we are going to have a big day ahead of us. Maybe we should get to bed early."

"That might be a good idea. Would you like to tuck me in?" I practically begged. Gina got up and walked over to me. She pulled my chair out and sat on my lap, gently grabbing my chin. Aw, shit this is it!

"I've been thinking about backing this thang up on it for a while," she murmured seductively.

I smiled slightly, rubbing my chin as I glanced over Gina, "The hell you say?" Gina was playin' it cool too, pretending not to notice my knee bouncing up and down like an addict in front of a Scarface size pile of coke. "Yeah, it's just I'm very selective about who I take to my bed. I need to know I can trust you."

"You definitely can trust me."

"Good boy."

We kissed, I'm on fire, damn she felt good. Gina got up, patted her butt, and growled, "Here boy."

"She had me. Oh man, she looked so good in that red dress. Her ass was boomin, her titties thick and juicy. I'm about to hit this like it's the last coochie on Earth, I thought to myself as I followed her to the bedroom.

She walked into the bathroom and shut the door. I bit my bottom lip and pulled out a strip of twenty condoms, a tube of KY jelly, a pair of pink feathered handcuffs, a string of anal beads, a pair of nipple clamps, a small whip, and a bottle of Mrs. Butterworth. I was ready for the showdown at the ho'down. I put everything on the nightstand, stripped, and hopped into bed.

The bathroom door opened and Gina walked out in a pink nightie. She rubbed her hands across her body and slowly moved toward the bed. "Are you ready for me, Mr. Thompson?"

"Damn, you sexy. Oh yeah I'm ready." I ain't never been harder in life! I was throbbin' so hard it's like my dick is having a seizure!

Gina crawled onto the bed and hovered over me. She kissed me all over as she straddled my waist. I'm ohhing and awing like I was having a contraction. She slid her hands onto her shoulders and began to pull down the straps of her nightgown. My foot was twitchin' so bad the back the headboard is bangin' against the wall at the sight of her deliciously plump cappuccino brown breasts.

My cell phone rang; I threw it out the room.

Gina grabbed my hands and placed them on her butt squeezing it as she traced a path over my body with her tongue. I flipped her over and flickered my tongue over her chest. The sweet salty taste of her sweat, laced with her perfume flooded my senses as I paid special attention to her quarter sized dark chocolate nipples. Nine months without a woman, I couldn't wait no more! I slid down to savor the sweet taste of her thighs making my way to her lips in between. The taste from her unshaven flower sent erotic pulses to through my body, begging me to caress her with my tongue. She smiled and grabbed my head trying to fill my mouth. Twenty minutes passed. I rose and licked my lips as I looked down on her body convulsing from the orgasm. I kneeled down and growled to grabbed Gina's waist, pulling toward me. She stopped me.

"Naw, Baby let me get it. I want to please you. You just relax."

"Oh, damn, you making my toes curl," I groaned. "I'm about to explode."

Gina stood up over me. "Get in the bed," she said, "and I'll be right back."

"Where you goin?" I asked, not believing she was leaving me in such pain.

"I want to let you inside every inch of me. I want you to use me until you get out of bed. And when you're done … ."Gina rubbed her breasts, stopping to pinch her nipples."… I want you to wake up and do it again. I'll be back."

AW SHIT! I got into bed and peeked under the covers looking at my dick. "I need you now like I have never needed you before. You need to go to the left, then to the right, I want you to bob and weave, stick and move, damnit. Stick and move!"

"Who you talking to, Baby?" Gina called out from the bathroom.

"Nobody. Come on out girl!"

"All right, close your eyes tight. I'm coming out all natural, and I'm a little self-conscious."

I closed my eyes as tight as I could and rocked in the bed. Gina dimmed the lights.

"Damn girl, show me what you got." I bit my bottom lip hard. I was about ready go into spasms'. "Aw, Baby I'm gonna put your damn back out!" she said. "Ooooh, baby, I like the sound of that. Open your eyes."

Just as I slowly opened my eyes slowly, ready to cover her body in ecstasy, Gina's fuckin' ass jumped on top of me dressed in a motherfuckerin doggie mascot suit!

"Woof, woof!", She yelped.

I laid in absolute shock as Gina barks and wags her tail. She raised up, and I looked this crazy

214

bitch over. My mouth and stomach dropped at the sight of the nightgown, bra, and panties over the suit!

"What the … are you … what the … what the hellv… Gina what is this?"

Gina yelped in response.

"What the fuck is this? Are you crazy? Gina, what the hell?"

In the truck, Michael gets out of the truck and falls over laughing on the ground. Kyle stares in shock.

"What do you mean? I don't understand." Kyle asks.

"She came out in a fuckin' dog suit.

"You mean like a sexy Playboy bunny type … "

"No, like a fuckin' Six Flags, grocery store grand opening, Kiddieland, kid's birthday party, freakin' doggie mascot!"

Outside, Michael wheezes for air.

"I hope you choke!" I yell through the window. "This shit ain't funny!"

Kyle wipes his face. "A dog?" he asks.

"Yes, a freakin' dog."

"Woof, woof kind of dog?" Kyle asks.

"Came out lookin like Bow Wow Benji, the scraggly ass fuckin' mutt."

Michael gets back into the truck panting, "Okay, I'm cool. What in the hell did you do?"

In the bedroom, Gina turned her head to the side and whines sadly. The doggie head is so fuckin' big that it's like one of those bobblehead toys. She began to beg like a dog and rubbed her floppy cloth tongue against my chest.

I'm not understanding this shit, somebody needed to explain this to me! All I know was that I was mad. I pushed Gina up off me. She flopped back down, bouncing the huge oversized doggie head off my chest. "This ain't doing shit for me. What the hell? Is this a joke?" I demanded.

Gina raised up and started talking through the dog head. "You said you like puppy play? What's up?"

"I thought you meant we gonna do it doggie style?"

"Oh okay … I can do that." Gina hopped up and gets on all fours. She moved the tail, sticking out of the G-string, out the way with her paw. She yelped as she bounced her doggie butt. "Woof … woof!"

Michael wipes the sweat from his forehead. "Please, please, please, tell me you didn't hit it. Tell me you didn't."

I lay my head on the steering wheel, "Man … "

Kyle scoots up toward us, "Well did you?"

"We ain't talking about me, we talking about Michael."

Michael snickers. "Did you grab her ears when you hit it?"

"Man, fuck you," I grouse.

Kyle snorts. "Did you scratch her belly and give her a milk bone when you finished? Did you chase her around with a chuck wagon?"

"Keep on, you'll be the limp dick havin'est motherfucker in Indy."

"So what you gonna do? You put nine months into this. You gonna walk away or you gonna be this bitch's man?" Michael asks, snickering again.

"I don't know, man. I mean the vibe is cool. She fine as hell, she's smart, she's about to get her master's next spring, she got her own house, own car, she's a million ways sexy, and we have a cool-ass time together. I almost didn't even mind waiting for it. But damn, this doggie shit is some … Shit! What's next?"

Michael rubs his chin, "Shit, I don't know what to tell you, Dude."

"I say you fuck her and the rest of the pound," Kyle suggests.

"You got one more time, Kyle!" I warn.

"Man, I'm just playin'. I'm playin'."

"A'ight, A'ight, A'ight. I'm gonna get back on you later. What we gonna do about this tape?"

"A'ight I know what I'm gonna do," I tell them. "Ya'll carry on with business as usual. Leave your cell phones on, and I'll be in touch."

"What's the plan?" Michael asks.

"Leverage," I say. "I'll be back."

Michael and Kyle step out of the truck.

"You just make sure that speech for tomorrow is tight and make sure that there are no changes for tomorrow. I'm going to see my boy Charlie."

"Charlie?" Michael asks.

"Yeah Charlie Daniels, my boy who used to work for Channel 7. He has his own private television studio and does a lot of freelance work now, for weddings, birthday parties, shit like that."

"So what does that have to do with this?"

"You'll see. Work on that speech. Make sure you're ready to make a strong impression. We gotta hit the Cultural Expo and the Urban League hard. If we have any chance of winning, we have to do it there."

"A'ight, man. "If you need something, hit me up," Michael says. He and Kyle head into Headquarters as I start the truck.

I call on Charlie on the cell phone. "Hey man, it's X. I need a favor man, big time. I'm on my way over."

CHAPTER TWELVE

DOWN THE CORPORATE LADDER
JERRY

Ten years on the job and I thought I'd seen it all, but this time is different; this Thompson thang is a bitch. Eyes are all over this, and Theresa and I are right in the middle. That's cool though, I wouldn't have it any other way. If we play this thang right, it could be a career maker for both of us.

Right now, I'm on my way to see Dicklis; probably wants to give me some bullshit ass assignment, like washing his car, getting lunch, goin' to pick cotton out the fields. I can't stand that old, shuckin' and jivin,' Jim Crowe bastard. That's all right, I'm just biding my time, waiting to make that move. Let's see what this asshole wants.

I knock on the doorframe, "You wanted to see me, Mr. Dicklis?"

Dicklis picks up his jacket and heads to the door. "Yeah, Jerry. I need you to help me shoot the new promo for the station down at Market Square."

"No, problem, Sir. I'll get my gear."

I pick up my camera, and we head to the news truck. The sun's starting to go down over the city skyline. I look over and see Dicklis typing a text message on his phone. We get into the truck and head to Downtown Market Square.

"Take Meridian all the way down to 10th street," he says, picking his nose.
"But Boss, Market Square is ten minutes east of that. Wouldn't it be faster to take St. Clair?"

"No, there's only one way in because of the wind damage to the Hamburg Tower."

"All right, Sir."

"I tell you what, turn on west on 10th street to Illinois. I want to get a sandwich first, and why don't pick up my dry cleaning while we wait for traffic to die down?"

I knew this Dude was gonna make me a chauffeur! If I didn't need this gig, I'd cuss his ass out. I pull over to 10th street.

"Stop over there on in front of The Savoy first."

"They built this hotel up quick, huh, Sir?"

"Just pull over there."

I park the truck, and we get out and stare up at the massive hotel. This place is the crème de la crème, five stars easily. Dicklis walks around to my side and puts his musty-ass arm around my shoulder as he leads me down the street.

"Son, I'm taking you to an important meeting today. Just keep your mouth shut and ears open, and maybe you'll learn something."

"Do I need to get my camera, Sir?"

"No, this is sort of a undercover expose.'. …It's, what do the colored kids say, on the D.L."

I roll my eyes. "Okay, Sir."

We walk behind The Savoy where a stretch black limo sits at the end of the alley. The license plate on it says RM Enterprises. Manning, I should have known the set up was on. The window rolls down and blue smoke pours out as the driver opens the door. He looks more like a bouncer at a Harlem juke joint, especially with the .45 caliber handgun shoulder holstered in his jacket. We slip inside of the limo, and the driver starts the motor, taking off out of the alley. I've never seen Manning up close before. His 6'6 350 lbs physique screams nothing but absolute power. Behind the shadow that seems to call his face home, his smoothly shaved head that is behind his cigar has the commanding respect of a Don.

"Hello, Mr. Wiley. Can I call you, Jerry?"

"Ye ... ye ... yes, Sir."

"Jerry, do you know who I am?"

"Of course, I do. You're Mr. Rex Manning."

"Good. Your boss tells me that you and Theresa Gomez have been working together on a number of stories over the last year."

"Yes Sir, we've worked on a number of projects together."

"I also heard you're one of the best cameramen in the city."

"Well, I do what I gotta do."

"I'm sure you do. You know, Jerry, I've been in the political game in Midwest for over thirty years. Shit, I was in the trenches before you were even out of diapers."

"I'm sure."

"You know the cool thing about this city, Jerry?"

"Hmm?"

"It is the crossroads of America, boy. We got playas from Chi-Town trying to bring that flava down here, trying to come up on come up, start up they own operation. Shit, half the time they trying to run away from the shit they done got started up there. Then we got the brothers from down south trying to see how us up north homies do it. But I tell you what, no matter where you come from there's gonna be a moment that the type of man you are shows; it's just a matter of time. Whether you be a bitch or a baller, take that first hit, get that first fat wad of cash, or have that first taste of platinum pussy. The Dude you are is gonna show, and that's when you gonna find me.

One thing I've learned on my time on this Earth is how to read people. I learn what people need. You hear me, not what they want but what they need. Then once I know that, I present the opportunity for them to go after it and get it. Shit, humph … Im practically a saint. I've gotten three keys to the city, awards from some of the most prestigious clubs in the Midwest, and tasted some of the finest women on the planet. Now you, Jerry, I can tell you a hustler. You got a plan, all you need is a door to open up, and you gonna make that move. Frankly, I'd like to make sure that a deserving brotha like yourself can get a door or two open to get yours."

"Now, why would you wanna do that?" I ask with a slight smirk.

"Cause, man, we one in the same. Don't let da Yves Saint Laurent, two thousand dollar suit and Cuban cigar fool you. I'm a straight hood rat who got a deal a long time ago. I'm just trying to pass along a little good Karma."

"So what is it that you want in return?" I ask.

Manning laughs. "Straight and to the point, my man. I've been talking to Mr. Dicklis here, and if you wanna stay in the television game, maybe we can get you some higher paid assignments, put you in charge of a few camera crews, maybe give you some time in front of the camera, so you can really blowup. Why should these white boys have all the fun? It's our turn."

"You still didn't answer my question."

"What do I want?"

"Yes?"

"See the political game and street game is the same motherfucka. I want friends. No, I want loyal friends, people that's gonna have my back, like I have theirs."

"I'm sure you got plenty of friends. What do you need with me?"

"This Theresa Gomez … " Manning's blows a long stream of smoke as we turn another corner, "… she ain't like us, she ain't from the hood. She's a college girl, a bookworm. She don't understand the world outside the textbook, the real world.

Sometimes you gotta get your hands dirty, put in a little work, scratch a back or two or somebody might put a knife in yours. Brothas like you and me couldn't afford to go to Harvard, Princeton or, uh, where'd she graduate from Dicklis?"

"Columbia."

"Yeah, Columbia. We don't have the advantage of a Brooks Brotha's, silver spoon education so our interests ain't the same as hers. What I want, is to know what's this big expose on Thompson. See I have a speech in an hour, and I need to know if I need realign my platform."

"So if I scratch your back … "

"I'll scratch yours. Thompson's the same way, an educated brotha like Gomez. He don't understand how this game works. Okay, he's got good ideas, but ideas don't mean a damn thing without the balls and power to back that shit. A lot of people like you and I are gonna get shitted on if that man gets elected. Things are gonna be run ass-backwards while he's trying to chase a dream. Martin Luther King had a dream, and what do we got now. Half the city in poverty, and guess which half? The darker half. See I'm like brotha Malcolm, 'By any means necessary!' You feel me Youngblood?"

"I hear what you saying. I feel you."

"So you see, we gotta stand together as a people. When I see a brotha in need, I feel compelled to lend a hand. Wrong flip of the card, and in two, three years that could be me. You help me out, and I won't forget you as a friend. If you wanna get into something new I need a public relations manager, someone in touch with how things really are on the street from my perspective, seventy-five thousand a year, BMW for a company car. I'd hate to steal you from Mr. Dicklis, but I'm sure he'll understand." Manning extends his hand, and I cut my eyes over to Dicklis who nodding his head up and down in approval.

"Mr. Manning, I'd like to help you, but I have to be honest. I'm just a cameraman. I took mostly raw footage for Theresa, she pieces it together. I'm as clueless as you."

Mr. Dicklis leans forward, "We understand that, but you're close to her. You can always find out and give us a call before the speech."

"And there's your door, my friend." Manning says blowing smoke.

I consider Manning's offer. "I could see myself behind a BMW," I say. " I tell you what, I'll see what I can do and get back to you, okay?"

"All right my speech is at six o clock. Get back at me. Cool?"

"Cool." I say shaking Manning's hand.

Manning laughs, "My Nigga! That's my Nigga, right, Dicklis?"

"Yeah, that's you huh ni…your nigger." Dicklis nervously lights a cigarette.

Manning laughs, and the limo pulls over next to the news van. Dicklis and I hop into the van and head back to the truck. I gotta talk to Theresa, I knew this election was gonna have something big in store for me.

CHAPTER THIRTEEN

AN ALL DAY ASS WHOOPIN' CHARLIE

I rush over to Charlie's place, hoping he will be able to come through for me. Charlie was always the first brotha to be down in a pinch. Although Charlie was white, he was an honorary brotha. We had a ceremony and everything to bring him in. Out of everybody in my crew in high school, Charlie was the first to start some shit and the last to leave. He was a mad scientist, Dr. Jekyell and Mr. Hyde, a thug with a Fortune 500 work ethic.

Like all of us, Charlie eventually grew up. He graduated first in his class at tech school, first in his class in undergrad, and top ten in graduate school. He even went on to marry one of the finest sistas in high school, Amanda Willis. Man, you talking about brothas being pissed, but everybody knew they bet not say shit cause this Dude was more bananas than Chiquita. I mean he was crazy. I ain't talking homeboy crazy, where some shit may get started over a scuffmark on some fresh Jordans. I ain't talking about white boy crazy where he'd be mad for something that happened in first grade go home, not say shit for eleven years and then on senior prom night blow up the school dressed in a pink tutu, combat boots, and a "I love Mama" T-shirt. Noooo, I talkin' white homie crazy, which was like Armageddon incarnate.

I always knew it was important to keep a tech head on the squad, and man did I have a job for him. I pull up to Charlie's driveway and notice him through his garage window. I get out, walk up, and knock on the door. The automatic garage door opens slightly as Charlie peeps out from underneath.

I giggle lookin' at this nut, "Charlie what you doing?" I ask.

Looking left and then right, Charlie whispers, "You by yourself, X?"

"Yeah, man, what's up?"

"Nothing man, roll under."

"Roll under? What you mean? What you doin'?"

"Man, come on and roll under the door." I don't know what's goin' on. Ain't no telling with this Dude, so I figure I'll play along. I roll under the garage door to see this fool wearing only a pair of black penny loafers, fire engine red tube socks, and Spongebob yellow boxers. "Dude, what the hell are you doin'?"

"Anybody follow you, Man?"

"No, Man. What up!"

"Keep your voice down!"

"A'ight, Man, a'ight. what's up? Somebody after you?"

"Yeah, yeah something like that," Charlie says looking out of the garage window. He ducks down as a pair of headlights shine past the door. "Turn dat light off! Turn it off!"

I turn off the light and I duck down. Shit, I don't know what this Dude has gotten me into, so I crawl over and whisper, "You acting like a crackhead. What's up? You got some bangers after you?"

"Naw, Man," Charlie says watching the car turn around in the cul-de-sac.

"What, the cops? You got warrants?"

"Naw, Dude. Shhh ... "

"Then what? The military, the mob, aliens, Pookie da clown, what?"

"Naw, Man. Manda."

"Who?"

"A-man-da"

"You out here looking like Lester da Molester because of your damn wife? Oh shit! You been creepin'?"

Charlie squints his eyes, looking outside. "What? Naw, Man, naw."

"What, you lose some money at the track?"

"No, nothin' like that."

I get up and flip back on the light. "Then why we out here, man?" I ask.

Charlie walks over to his full sized pickup and opens the bedgate. We sit down on the edge.

"Man, you know those T.V. relationship experts types always say shit like, 'communication is one of the most important parts of a healthy marriage'?"

"Yeah, something like that, I guess."

"Well man, don't believe that shit cause miscommunication is a bitch!"

"Okay, what happened?"

"The other night, me and Amanda were having our usual Friday night 'Red Shoe Diaries', time. I'm hittin' it like I'm tryin' to make a baby, and she turns the T.V. on to the damn Home Shopping Network. She even had the audacity to put the remote on my back, crack open a Pepsi, and call in an order. I'm trying to give her the red light special, and she on the phone orderin' freakin' Gaucho Boots on sale. She even asked me to reach over and get her damn purse so she can grab her Visa."

"Aw Man, that's jacked up."

"Jacked up? Fucked up is what is!" He looks raises up trying to see out the garage door window. "So you know she da manager at RW Financial down on Fifth?"

"Right, right."

"Shoot, all type of big ballers be comin' in there tryin' to holla at her. Shit, I figure I gotta do something. Next thing you know, she'll be playin' solitaire on my ass while I'm layin' the pipe."

"So, what happened? Somebody stepped to o'girl, and you got in a fight?"

"Shit, I wish. I came up with this little idea on how to Spice things up ... "

Last weekend, I went to Club Paris on Illinois for The Silky, Sexy, Saturday Night Party. It was a cool little vibe. Enough dimes to fill a bank, and I'm there on the top floor of the place with my boy Sean shooting some Eight Ball. I looked over to the stairs in the corner of the room and saw this pack of honeys walking up on the floor. You know the drill, automatically some bustas already there tryin' to get wit it. Anyway, Amanda popped out of the group and came up to the table. Truth be told, she was fine … I mean like Tyra Banks, runway model fine. I ain't seen her this hot in years. She's wearing this tight little leather outfit, high heel thigh high boots, fishnets, the whole nine. She stepped up to the end of the table and watched me line up a shot. I was trying to focus on the game, but her legs was bangin' in that leather mini. She walked over to the rack and grabbed a pool cube. My eyes were just stuck on her toned arms flexing in her skin-tight top.

"Eight ball side pocket." I said, tapping the ball in. "That's game, Dude." I smile as I grab my mug and take a sip of beer. I looked Amanda up and down and smiled, "Hey, how *you* doing?"

Amanda took a sip of red wine. "I'm good, real good. What ya'll playin' for?"

"Aw, naw, we just playing for fun."

"For fun?" she asked.

I licked my lips. "Yeah for fun. You wanna play a game?"

"I don't know; I play better if there is something at stake," she said.

"Really?

"For sho." Her raspberry lips part a devious smile.

"So, what? You gonna try to hustle me?"

"No but I can play for fun anytime. I want something different tonight. Let's make it interesting, best two out of three. If I win, you buy me and my girls a bottle of Kyris."

"And if I win?"

"You can take me home and do any and everything little you … " Amanda kneels to pick up the cue ball rack off the floor, stopping short to graze her nails across the pounding Johnson in my jeans, "… and your little friend can think of."

I reached in my pocket to take out a money clip full of twenties. "Oh, I can handle that wager," I boasted. I smiled smugly and threw the money clip on the table. "Rack 'em up, Gal."

We played for about an hour. Honestly I forgot Ol'Girl could shoot as good as she could. I have to admit she kept me on my toes, but I wasn't gonna let the kitty get away that easily. After the making the last shot, I smiled and tossed the pool cube on the table. I lit a cigar as Amanda took a huge swig of wine.

"It looks like that's game," she said.

Amanda sat down at the stool in the corner of the room, biting one of her fingernails, tryin' to play the naughty, innocent girl routine. "Give a girl a second chance. How about one more game?" she implored.

I walked over to her, rubbing my hands together, "Naw, I'm gonna take this victory," I said trapping her in the corner, placing my arms against the wall on both sides of her. "So it looks like we have a debt to settle." I leaned into her neck, but she placed her hand on my chest to stop my advance.

"All right then, meet me outside, and we'll settle up," Amanda said, slipping out of my trap. She grinned, motioning with her index finger for me to "come here," as she sashayed down the stairs. She disappeared through the crowd on the dance floor.

As I made my way outside the club, I heard the sound of a motorcycle revving. I looked around to see where the sound was coming from and seconds later. Amanda pulled up next to me. "If you want this booty, you better hurry up," she ordered and skidded away. I sprint to my bike, start the engine, and took off after her.

Amanda raced down the street like she just robbed a damn bank, but I followed laughing all the way. She flew down the Interstate, weaving in and out the traffic, passing car after car at eighty-five, ninety miles per hour while I was just tryin' to keep up with her. When she got to open road, she popped a wheelie and opened up the engine like a bat out of Hell on fire. She had to be going like a hundred, maybe hundred ten; so I was getting nervous. I started weaving slightly, trying keep my balance to catch up with her. Amanda made a sharp turn onto another Interstate exit, and I skidded across traffic trying not to lose her. Amanda launched her bike off the ramp and onto the highway. A car pulled in front of my bike forcing me to pull the brakes. I skidded to the left and right. Car horns blew as I fought to keep from layin' the bike down. Amanda looked back, I guess she felt pity for my ass. She slowed down to merge onto the shoulder. I pulled over onto the shoulder and got off the bike.

"Damnit, Amanda! You tryin' to fuckin' kill me?"

"Aw, poor baby … I thought you was ready for a real ride. I tell you what, Boy, if you want some of this, you better put your ass in gear." She peeled away, spraying gravel and smoke behind her. I hopped on my bike, ready to catch her ass …

"Man, it sounds like ya'll were having fun."

"Yeah, it was. I followed her home, and I'm thinking this is great, just what we needed to get the blood pumpin'. I felt exhilarated and horny as hell …

We got home, parked the bikes, and went at it right in the garage. I ripped off her clothes, she snatched off mine, and we about fuck like its 1999. I got her pinned up with her back to me against the side of my truck. She's screaming, I'm screaming, we ain't had sex like this in years. I'm diggin' in so deep, I had her growling. I gripped the bed rail, trying to hold on to my sanity, the outside windows are fogged up, and the truck is rocking. Shit, I wish she would try to grab the damn phone now …

"God, you feel good, Boy. Riding down the street, with that huge engine revving between my thighs got me so fuckin' hot!"

"Damn girl! Shit, I can tell"

"I want you to hit like it's the last pussy on Earth."

She ain't said nothin' but a thang. A brotha had to tap dat ass proper. I had to. I grabbed her hips and moaned as I pressed deep inside her pushing her on her toes. The sight of her breasts pressed against the truck window sent warm waves of hunger down my body. She smiled and bit her bottom lip. I couldn't let her get away with that, she put me through too much shit. I had to hear her. Shit, I wanted the whole neighborhood to hear my damn name. I leaned in and let my lips make love to her neck, her weak spot. Her lips quivered a sexy smile …

"Charles! Oh! Take me Charles!! Take it!" Amanda said, gripping the truck, and leaning her head back. "Smack my ass and call me a bad girl."

I spanked dat ass. "You've been such a bad girl," I told her. "You been so bad. Is this how bad girls like to be fucked?"

"Oh yes…fuck…yes! Get it, get it!"

My arm and chest muscles tightened as I pushed harder. "This the way you want it? Huh? Huh!"

Amanda pushed back. "Yeah, yeah. Call me a bad girl. I've been so fuckin' bad! Yes!"

I wipe d the sweat pouring from my face. My heart pounded faster, so loud I could hear it echo in my ears. Amanda grabbed her left breast, thrusting back harder. Our bodies moved like a well-oiled machine ready for an eruption.

"Get it, white boy, get it! Grab my hair!! I've been soooo bad! Don't stop! Don't you dare stop!"

"Yeah, yeah! You like this, you bad girl?"

"Oh YEAH! I like it boy! Keep it up! Harder! Tell me I've been bad!"

I pushed like there's no tomorrow.

"Yeah, boy! God I needed this! Get it! Get it! This is what I've been waiting for! Call me a bitch!"

"Yeah, you bitch, take it!" I said as I enjoyed the sweet taste of her sweat from her shoulders.

"Yeah like that, keep goin! Oh damn, I'm almost there!! Ooh Fuck! Yes!"

"Yes! Yes! You like this you nasty bitch? Cum on these big balls you…you dirty ass, gutterslut, stank ass, cunt bitch! Yeah! Yeah, you fuckin' ho!"

Amanda stopped and turned around, "Wait… wait … wait a minute what did you just say?"

"Huh?" My mouth dropped.

"Nigga I ain't tell you to say all *that* shit!" As soon she said that it was like somebody put my dick in the icebox. She pushes me out and proceeded to kick, no beat my ass. I mean it was an all day, L.A.P.D. ass whoopin.' It was like getting beat in shifts."

"Come on it couldn't have been that bad man. Amanda's like what 4'11?"

"Yep."

"You what 6'5?"

"6'5, 275 pounds."

"And you a third degree belt in Karate."

"It was a fourth degree whoopin'. I mean it was like fighting the Matrix, like someone ownloaded some Kung Fu in her head. Dude, it was crazy, it was like a squirrel fucking up a bear over a nut. I couldn't even get my pants up. I tried to run upstairs, but this chick chases me down and slams into the bikes, tackling me like a linebacker stopping a touchdown. She took me out at the knees! I had to get up and run down the street in my damn draws. Shit, I thought she was gonna kill me! I can't even go back in the house, I've been livin' out here in the garage since Saturday. Ain't no phone out here, my cell in the house. I can't drive, my keys went down a street drain when she threw them at me in the street.

She took the clothes I wore from the club. I tried to sneak in the house a couple of times, but she's right there waitin'. I'm hungry and cold. Can I get a hug, Dude?"

"Dude, I ain't huggin' you in your damn draws." I try to hold in my laughter at this fool. "Man, don't worry I'm gonna try and hook you up, but first I need a solid. Mike has got himself in some deep shit. I got an idea, but it is gonna take your special touch. Peep this ... ."

CHAPTER FOURTEEN

THE RALLY
THERESA

Seven-Thirty P.M. Damn, I'll be happy when this day it over with. I can't wait to sit back and take a long hot bath. I head to my office to take a powernap before the Inside Scoop broadcast at eleven-thirty. I lock the door, turn off the light, and feel the snore coming on when a voice calls over the intercom, "Theresa … Theresa … Theresa. Are you in?"

I turn on the lights. "Yes, Mr. Dicklis."

"Please come to my office ASAP!"

"Yes, sir on my way." Dammit, what could he want now? Shit! Putting on my best trooper face, I walk over to his office. I knock on the door ready for another dose of his sour mash bullshit. All I know is I better not hear another thing about Manning, or I'm gonna snap.

"Theresa, please come in. Look, I need you to cover a breaking story downtown. There is an immigration rally going on in the Circle. Have you heard anything about it?"

"I've heard a couple things about officials planning a protest, but I didn't know if anything would ever come of it, in Indianapolis at least."

"Apparently there's a large support base for the rally here. Police estimate about a thousand supporters marching downtown. It's been real hush-hush. The police weren't even prepared for the numbers. I need you to go down there and cover it for the 10 o'clock newscast. Be sure to get a lot of on the street interviews. I really want to hit this as a people interest story. I'm thinking about running a personal profile of a different immigrant every night for a week, so try to make a lot of contacts. I want to see it from the eyes of the protesters. "

"No problem, Boss. Where is Jerry?"
"He should be on his way back from Manning's speech. If he hasn't made it back, take Anna. She could use some experience. Let's see, all the vans are taken so take my SUV. Take one of the

Portable Investigation Units and be careful. That's my baby." He tosses me the keys and I head to my office to gather my materials. I walk out to the lobby and see Jerry walking back in from the Manning assignment.

"Hey, Jerry. Man, you got time to head out downtown to cover that Immigration Rally."

"Yeah, let me just hit the head, and I'll be right there." He leans into my ear, "Man, I gotta tell you about my meeting with Manning."

"Aw shit, you met the great Rex Manning, huh?"

"Yep, it was a trip. I'll tell you on the way."
"Cool."

"I'll be back." Jerry heads to the bathroom. I see Mr. Dicklis in the reflection of the office windows in the back of the lobby. He grabs Jerry's arm hard and says something to him. I can't make it out, but Dicklis's pissed off! Jerry snatches his arm away and stares him up and down. They look at each other like they ready to square off. Jerry turns his back going to the bathroom, still halfway staring at Dicklis. I step closer to see what's going on, but Dicklis heads my way. I play it off, grabbing my cell phone to check my messages. A few minutes pass and Jerry comes back out.

"What's up with you and Dicklis?"

"Fuck if I know. He's a bitch sober. I can't stand that bastard."

"I know, man, I know. Just a few hours to go and this day will be done."

"Shit, I can't wait hit the bed tonight!"

"You ain't lying boy. Lets go handle this and get something to eat for dinner, my treat."

CHAPTER FIFTEEN

THE TALE OF THE
TAPE
XAVIER

It's on. I look at my watch as I arrive to the Channel 10 studio, seven-thirty. I park the truck, turn on the cabin light, and pull down the visor to check myself out in the mirror. I straighten my tie, brush my mustache, push the visor back up, and step out of the truck smoothing out my suit jacket and pants. I know what I'm about to do is pretty grimy, but let's be honest to get a rat sometimes you gotta go into gutter. Kyle's comment about that porno chick Ava Dennis looking like Theresa gave me an idea; a tape of my own to get a little leverage against Theresa's tape of Michael.

Charlie and I were able to take one of Ava Dennis' old tapes and superimpose her image with a brotha that we'll say was Michael. We even placed a tattoo on Ava's back like the one Theresa has on her back. It's a gamble, but I was able to get my boy Charlie to doctor a tape of them having sex on my oak table, the one Michael says looks like the one Theresa and him had sex on for his birthday. The plan is that if she goes on with the story at eleven-thirty I'll release the doctored tape on the Internet by eleven forty-five. I even set up a web page, www.tackeytelaho.com, and Charlie set up an account, which will send the video to a thousand webmasters in the U.S. By this time tomorrow, it will be on over ten thousand PC's the world over. That might cause a problem with this new position as an evening anchor position she's been offered. Since C.N.N. doesn't stand for Clit N' Nuts she may wanna take this deal to let go of her tape so I can get rid of mine.

Shit, even if she sues, it will be months before we see a courtroom and how many PC's will it be on by then; tens of thousands? She'll be a household name. She lives for the spotlight, let her have it. Like I said, it was a grimy plan, but if she take my brother's campaign, I'll take her career. She may not go for it all together, but it's worth a shot.

248

This is it. Its not about the damn Election Day, it's about tonight, his career skyrockets or crashes right now. Fuck her, either she gives up Mike's story ,or I'll make sure the only position she has on T.V. is on her back.

I grab my briefcase and head for the front door. In the distance, I notice Theresa on her way up the parking lot.

"Theresa! Theresa Gomez just a second! Theresa!" I scream trying to get her attention as I jog over to her.

"Oh, Xavier Thompson, nice to see you again. This is Jerry, my cameraman."

"Nice to meet you, man." I shake Jerry's hand.

Theresa smiles, "Well, you look quite dashing this evening. How can I help you?"

"I was hoping to speak with you in private for a moment."

Theresa checks her watch. "Well we're one our way out to cover a story."

"I only need a minute," I say.

"All right, sixty seconds."

"I was hoping that you would reconsider about the news broadcast about Michael."

"I'm sorry. The wheels are already in motion. It's slated as our local special feature."

"Look, he can do a lot of good of our community. There's no need to … "

"You look," she interrupts. "I've heard the spiel before. What's done is done; I've made my decision. If Mike is such an asset to the community, the voters will still elect him."

"But what is the point of embarrassing him. Let's keep the issues the main focus, not a one time incident in his personal life."

"I'm not a politician, Mr. Thompson, I'm a journalist. My job is to report the news, period. I'm not gonna play favorites to Manning or your brother."

"And there is no such thing as, uh, selective reporting, passing up stories for better, more important ones?"

"True, but I don't see the need to exclude this one. Look, I'd like to be able to help you but my hands are tied. We have the complete story, and we are going to tell it. If you will excuse me, I have work."

"Just hold on a second … "

Jerry steps in front of me, "Look, man, that's it, don't make me call Security."

"A'ight, man, I'm cool."

Theresa and Jerry begin to walk away.

"Oh, no, I'm not through with you by a long shot. I don't care if I have follow you into Hell, I'm not letting Mike's career go down with fight," I whisper to myself. I head back to my truck to follow them to their next story. I decide to hang back so they won't know which car is mine. I can't afford them making me out as a tail on the road. I bend down and pretend to tie my shoe, to try to disappear from sight. Theresa's heels click loudly on the wet pavement. Her movements, slowly and graceful are still hypnotizing as she walks to her car. I focus in on them. Something's wrong. My eyes squint, my fingers touch the ground, posed like a track star ready to go for the gold. I start to walk kneeling low to the ground. My walk turns into a sprint and then a mad dash. My heart's on fire.

"Theresa! Hey Theresa wait up!"

"Damn, what does this fool want!" Theresa says, stopping to turn to look at me. Her words register in slow motion in my brain. "Go on ahead and load the equipment in, I'll get rid of him."

She tosses the keys to Jerry and turns around to me.

"HEY MAN, HOLD ON!!" I scream as Jerry pushes a button on the remote. The lights flash. I jump out to grab Theresa. The SUV explodes.

CHAPTER SIXTEEN

FACES

XAVIER

My eyes open to the heavens. The night sky is filled with smoke. I lift myself off the ground, glass is all over me. My head is doing the Rumba as I look around, faces everywhere, some cryin,' most just in shock. The sound of a fire engine's siren is cutting gashes in my skull. My eyes burn from the heat of the flames burning off the cars around me. I gotta know what's going on.

My chest feels like its gonna cave in as I cough out the black smoke in the air. Hell, it looks like I made out better than Jerry. My eyes watch him as they put the blanket over his body. His corpse looks like its gonna be smoking for a week. Poor bastard, he never knew what hit him. My eyes search for Theresa. I guess someone else wanted to make sure that she didn't go on the air tonight. Who am I kidding, there's only one man in this town with the muscle to pull off a hit like this. Even if Manning wasn't responsible, no body makes a major move without him knowing it; his political power and underbelly stretches way too far without him having any information about the hit. I gotta find out the real deal.

I crawl over to Theresa, lying on the ground reaching for her purse. She grabs a medallion of the Virgin de Guadalupe and hands it to me. She mumbles trying to stay conscious. She asks me to hold on to it for her. Her eyes close as the EMT's surround us.

A sharp pain hits me as I notice the EMT's putting her covered body in the ambulance next to mine. Damn.

They close the doors to the ambulance and rush me to the hospital. I gotta get out of here. I need to deal with Manning before one of my family members or me wake up with a bomb under our car. The election ain't worth this. At the hospital, they wheel me in, and the doctor checks me out. I have a slight concussion, cracked rib, and a few bruises. They want me to stay overnight for tests. Sorry, I can't oblige.

The nurse dims the light in my room. I wait a few minutes and pull myself from the warm sheets and slowly place my feet on the cold marble floor. I walk over to the closet, slip on my clothes, and peek out of the door. Seeing a clear hallway fuels my retreat to the main waiting room. Outside the hospital I hail cab back to the studio.

Watching the lights of city, my mind spins as I try to stay focused on the goal at hand but thought of events of my life interrupt. Eventually focus cuts through the madness. Seeing my truck, I pay the cabbie, climb into the truck and place my throbbing head against the headrest. I watch the cab disappear among the flashing lights of the investigators still probing the scene of the explosion.

I wipe my eyes and drive to the drugstore to get about eight aspirins. I feel like I need a hundred, but I've got stay as sharp as possible. In the store, people stare at me, looking like I one of the walking dead. I grab the aspirin and a bottle of juice, placing it against my ribs. The cold bottle feels good against my wounds. I walk to the counter, trying not to draw more attention than I already am. The cashier is barely able to keep her eyes on the register for staring at me.

Eventually I make it back to my truck, slide in, and start the engine. I look to the rear view mirror. My eyes are so red I barely recognize them. In the backdrop, I notice the cross from the hospital behind me. I close my eyes and turn off the engine. The crucifix dangling from my rear view mirror taps against the vents on the dashboard as it always does. Today, it calls to me. I grab the long chain and wrap it around my hand. My head falls to the top on my steering wheel. My lips part and my heart opens.

"Father, I come to in need of guidance for tonight I have witnessed evil. I ask Father that you grant me sight so I can see the truth. Grant me the sight to see it and strength so I can exploit it. Grant me the sight to see weakness so I can avoid it. Father make my actions pleasing to your will, make my sword just. Please Father guild me through the valley of darkness so I can save my family. In Jesus name I pray. Amen."

I open the glove compartment, take out my .45, and check the clip. I slide the magazine back inside and pull back the slide action. I stuff it in the back of my pants and pull out of the lot.

I arrive at The Savoy. It's half past midnight, but Manning's limo is still parked in the front. Hopefully, he's still here. I have no clue how I'm gonna pull this off, but shit, I'm probably the last person he expects to see now, so at least I can get the drop on him. I walk to the front door; my hands shake as I reach to open the door.

"Breathe, X, breathe," I tell myself pushing the up button to the forty-seventh floor. The elevator door opens and immediately two big NFL linebacker lookin' brothas eye me up and down.

"Here we go." I say to myself walking to the front desk.

"Yo, my man, can I help you?" one of the linebackers asks.

"Yeah, I need to speak to Mr. Manning for a minute."

"Sir, our office is closed. You can make an appointment during our business hours, 8;30 AM to 6:00 PM. I'm afraid you'll have to come back during that time."

"I'm afraid my business with Mr. Manning is of an urgent manner."

"I'm sure it's not urgent enough to disturb Mr. Manning in the middle of the night. You will need to come back tomorrow," he warns, putting his huge paw on my arm.

"Look, I don't want any trouble; I just want a minute of his time."

"I'm gonna tell you one last time, Mr. Manning ain't going to meet nobody right now!" He slams his hand into my chest and grabs my shirt. I twist to the side and grab his hand. Peeling his fingers off my shirt, I joint lock them toward the back of his wrist. He buckles.

The other guard draws his gun. "Look, man, let him go, or you about to have a real bad night!"

"Do it, man! Please!!" The linebacker, on his knees with tears streaming down his face, screams.

"Just tell Manning that Xavier Thompson is here to see him. NOW!"

"You let him go. I ain't gonna ask you again!" The guard steps closer.

"Then you gonna have to shoot me and he is going have to learn to jack off with his left hand!"

"Ca … Ca … Call Manning. Do it now!" The linebacker screams, "Oh God! I think I'm gonna pass out!"

The guard dials a number on his cell phone. "Mr. Manning. this is Jaime at the front desk. I'm sorry to bother you, but there is a Mr. Xavier

Thompson here to see you regarding an urgent matter … Yes, Sir, I will send him right up." Jaime hangs up the phone. "This way, Sir."

I let the linebacker's hand go, and he gives me the evil eye as we head to Manning's office. We arrive at the office door and Jaime presses his hand against my chest hard, holding me back as the other one announces me opening the door.

"Mr. Thompson, a pleasure to meet you." Manning grabs my elbow and hand and shakes it. "Normally, I would offer my guests something but you must forgive me. You caught me at the end of my day. What can I do for you?"

I look around the office at the four guards in front of Manning's desk, "I'll cut to the chase. I know about the car bomb at the Channel 10 building tonight. I also know that you are the major player in town and that nothing happens in Indy without your John Hancock on the dotted line; which means that you either ordered the hit or you know who signed off on it."

"Go on … "

"It's also no secret that my brother has been the only man to stand in your way in a long time. If he wins the election, it's gonna cause a major hit to your wallet. I know you stand to make a large chuck of change off this community redevelopment deal, and Michael's in the way. Knowing that, it's not totally inconceivable that me or my family might wake up one day to a unpleasant surprise in our car or happen upon some other unfortunate accident. Frankly, I can't have that."

"Sounds like you've given this a lot of thought. So what do you want?" Manning says, shifting his eyes to his guards standing around his desk.

"I want insurance. I'll convince Michael to drop out of the race. We'll make an announcement at the Urban Christian League Rally on Saturday. In exchange, I want your word that no harm will come to me, Michael, or any of the rest of our family. We'll leave Indy and the city will be yours. It's as simple as that."

"And how do I know your brother will listen to you?"

"He trusts me. I'm his closest confidant. If I tell him it is in our best interest, he'll listen. He wouldn't put his family at risk. I give you my word on that."

" I will give you this you got a lot of balls coming up here. Ha! It's almost one o' clock in the morning, you looking like shit on Hell's wings, and you wanna negotiate. Well you stated the obvious, I do stand to make a major piece of change off this deal. Try about 150 million dollars. That ain't chump change, Son. You're right, too, Michael is the only obstacle to me flexing my political muscle to control those contracts, but have him drop out? I cannot do that. Hell, I'm banking 150 million dollars on him to win."

"What the hell are you talking about?"

"Why don't you explain it to him, man." Manning nods to my rear.

I look over my shoulder, "Michael!" I exclaim, shock written all over my face.

Pulling off his glasses, Michael walks into the office. "Xavier, what are you doing here?" he asks.

"I'm trying to convince Manning to spare our lives, but I guess I was wrong there's no need for that. How much man?"

Michael sits down on Manning's desk. Manning hands him a Cuban, and Jaime lights it, "Seventeen million," he coolly replies.

"So, that's the cost of your soul?"

"Yeah, it costs a pretty penny."

"Why, man? I thought you were going change things. I thought you were in to make a difference?"

"Let me tell you something about ideals, lil' Bro. They're fine and good for the bedtime stories we read to our kids at night, but in the real world, ideals don't mean Jack Shit without power and balls to back it up."

"So what, seventeen million is gonna give you the power and balls to do some good?"

"No it's just a seed. I put all of it aside to pump into the community. Not a penny is going in my pocket."

"And in the meantime, you gonna let Manning continue to rape Indy in the process? Violent crime is up, poverty, gang membership numbers increasing. I thought you cared about that."

"You ain't understanding, man. With that seed money, I can start a franchise of community after school centers, anti-gang programs, new jobs, scholarships, even a franchise of martial art schools for you help to keep kids off the street. I know it seems bad, but sometimes you gotta make strange bedmates to make things happen. Manning is one of the most powerful brothas in the city. With him in our corner we *can* make a difference."

"And what does he get in return by letting you win?"

Manning blows smoke in the air. "I need a new well known face to be the front man of this deal. Michael's gonna be the Mr. Squeaky Clean image of R.M. Enterprises. He's gonna handle thangs in the public eye from the front office while I quarterback thangs from the sideline counting the money. So while Michael is opening new rec. centers, revitalizing schools, and building low cost homes on the East Side; I'm going be taking my part off the top for my private ventures generating more revenue for the cause."

"And a tasty kickback from the government funds for you in the process?" I ask, fanning the smoke away.

"Don't ask questions you already know the answer to, Son."

Michael puts down his cigar. "Xavier, you're not seeing the big picture. Everybody can make money and get ahead on this deal. The East Side has been struggling for years. This way we can stop making promises and start funneling cash in the neighborhood to build it back up. Manning has even promised to keep forty percent of the revitalization area low rent so downtown workers can continue to live there."

"That's right." Manning winks at me.

"And you're gonna trust his word? Have you lost your mind? Do you know what this man is into? Do you know what he is gonna drag us into?"

"Look, everybody makes money on this deal … "

"So this whole fuckin' day, you've been playin' me! There was never any fire or crazy relationship between you and Theresa. Oh but there was a story, wasn't there? A special expose' on your campaign, but you had no idea what the subject was. This whole day you've been Spittin' Game, bullshittin' me to find out what dirt Theresa had on you."

Manning's grimy ass claps. "The last horse finally crosses the finish line."

"I'm sorry, Dude. I just had to be sure what was going on. I had to push you to find what she had. I knew that if you thought she had a personal vendetta, you would go all balls out to stop her." Grabbing my arm, Michael pleads with me. I snatch it away and lean back punching him in the jaw. He falls to the ground holding his bloody mouth. Manning's guards tense up, Manning waves his hand for them to relax. I stare at Michael struggling to get up.

"How could you play me like this! I trusted you! I believed in you! I love you and you play like a punk!"

"Xavier, I'm sorry. I figured no body would get hurt, and we would know if there was anything to be worried about."

"Do you know what the fuck I've been through today? Nobody would get hurt? Tell that shit to Theresa and her cameraman Jerry."

"What are you talking about?" Michael asks standing up.

"Car bomb at the Channel 10 studios."

"What!"

"Yeah, your partner in crime had his own way of making sure the story didn't go on tonight."

"What is he talking about, Rex? This was supposed to be a only on paper thang, no violence!"

"What did you expect me to do? I tried to bribe, sweet talk, and dazzle that bitch. She wouldn't move. I pumped in over one million dollars into that station and that bitch wanted to play hardball. She could have been exposing everything about you, everything we've got planned; which means she could exposing me, and that is a clear cut case of her or me, and you better believe, I'll take out her and a dozen other Nigga-Spic bitches that look like her before I go down. Don't be getting squeamish on me now, Thompson. You knew what I was when you got involved with me! Now, I know we don't have a problem … "

Manning pauses and takes out a freakin' hand cannon from his desk drawer. "… or do I have to let my partner Mr. .357 Magnum handle my negotiations from this point forward?"

Michael steps forward. "Ain't no need for that. We're cool."

Manning puts the gun on his desk, "Good, I'm glad to hear that. Now what we gonna do about Xavier?"

"I'll vouch for him. He'll get on board with our program. You have my word."

"What? Do I look like an idiot to you, Mike? I'm suppose to just let him walk out of here, knowing what he knows?" Manning asks.

I pull my piece and point it at Manning. "I don't think you gonna have much of a choice."

His guards pull their guns. Manning slowly puts his hands up. "Nigga, you must be crazy to pull your gun on me. That's a commitment you may not walk away from Dawg. I suggest you think it through before you get outed up in here."

"Xavier, put the gun down!" Michael screams.

"Shut the fuck up, Michael! Now this is how it is gonna go. I'm gonna walk out of here, and if anybody follows me they getting blasted!"

"There ain't no way in hell you gonna live to see the sunrise," Manning warns.

I cock the hammer on the pistol. "Then I'll guess I make sure you get it first!"

With his hands still up, Manning smiles at me and says, "A'ight. Go ahead, little man. I got dat ass. I'll see you soon."

I glance behind me and start walking out, making sure the front sight of my gun stays dead center of the middle of the bastard's eyes.

"Why don't you go with him, Michael, since you wanna vouch for his punk ass. Let me tell you something. If you think what I did to that bitch Theresa was something, I got a factory on the south side just for little Niggas like you. Do me a favor and run. Make it fun for me, cause I gonna savor skinning dat ass personally. Let that bitch go!"

The guards smile and lower their guns. I back out slowly with Michael behind me. My gun is still pointing at Manning's head ready to send him to Hell. We reach the back of the office. A loud crash startles me.

"Federal Agents! Everybody drop their weapons and get down!" A dozen FBI, and IRS agents smash in the door weapons drawn. "Manning-interlock your fingers on put them on top of your head. Walk slowly around to the front of the desk, drop to your knees, and cross your legs. NOW! Don't make me kill you!" An agent commands.

"A'ight man, be cool. Be cool." Manning replies, falling to the ground.

"You two, on the floor! Now!" Another agent commands Michael and me.

"Yes, Sir." I drop my gun in reply, and we slowly drop to the ground.

"No, not this one. He's with me." I look as a pair of heels click their way into the office. I look up to see scarred up Theresa, with one arm in a sling and the other holding a pistol.

"It's about time," I say.

"I'm sorry it took us so long, Xavier. There was a ten second delay on your transmission. Cheap ass Federal equipment,." she says throwing her earpiece down.

"Oh yeah, I suppose you will want this back." I stand up and take off the medallion with the mini recorder inside, "You got the evidence that you needed?"

"Oh, yeah, Baby. Oh yeah."

An agent picks Michael up. "So you were playin' me, lil bro?" Michael asks.

"Naw, man, I didn't know you were involved in this at all. This was just about Manning. I didn't even know she was a Fed. until the explosion.

"So, Miss Gomez, what was the story, then?" Michael asks.

"There wasn't one, but knew there was no part of the election Manning wasn't gonna want to control. I also knew that if there was gonna be a special expose' about his number one boy, he'd come out strong to try to control the game. Seventeen million in an off shore account, Michael. You need to learn funnel your money a little better, Bro. Take him downstairs."

When the agents stand Manning up, I walk over to him and say, "Looks like I got da ass."

"Nigga, all you did was buy your mama that black dress. I'll be out in a week!"

Theresa laughs, "Oh, I don't think so, racketeering, multiple violations of the R.I.C.O. statue, tax evasion, and attempted murder and premeditated murder of a Federal agent, my partner Jerry. Oh, no, my brother, you'll be going away for a long, long time. Not bad for a half Spic, half Nigger bitch huh? Take this punk ass, ghetto Al Capone, Nino Brown wanna-be down to the car."

CHAPTER SEVENTEEN

WHAT A DAY
XAVIER

I check my watch. Damn, two A.M. We all walk out single file to the Fed's vans and police cruisers waiting in front of The Savoy. I never thought the day would end like this, with Michael in handcuffs in front of me. The news vans pull up, and reporters jump out like ants over a cracked jar of honey. The flashes of the cameras blind me. It will be on television first thing in the morning.

A reporter breaks through the crowd; he looks as bad as me. I can't see his face, but I'm getting that slow motion feeling again. His coat opens; there's a .45 where his microphone should be. He fires a shot out from the crowd. The agent next to me falls down. Blood splatters on my face as I grab Theresa and throw her down. The second bullet whizzes by us hitting a reporter. Shot three, another agent falls. The agents try to return fire, but they are pinned down in the confusion. They can't get a clear shot.

The shooter pushes through the crowd, getting closer to us. He stands in front of one of the police cruiser's rear passenger windows. It becomes clear what he wants. He fires inside the police cruiser. Manning looks in horror as the bullets and glass violently rip the life from him.

The agents close in shouting orders for him to drop the gun as he looks around scene. News cameras roll, he smiles, straightens his tie as the camera flashes reflect off his bloodstained glasses. He places his piece to his head and fires. The agents close in guns drawn.

Theresa helps me up. "Dicklis. I guess he finally stopped livin' up to his name."

"But why?"

Theresa hands me a handkerchief. "Who knows. Maybe he was in deeper than anyone thought. Maybe he thought that he would be a target in Manning's retaliation campaign from behind bars because of someone fouling up the car bombing by wiring the bomb to the alarm instead of the ignition.

Hell, maybe he just had enough of being the pot that life pissed in."

"Yeah, whatever the reason, I'm sure the moment he saw that bastard tremble felt real good."

The agents secure the scene. Theresa and I walk to my truck. "So what now?" I ask, wiping off the blood from my face.

"Well, that's twice today you saved my life. If you hadn't of grabbed me, the bomb shrapnel would have killed me at the studio. And now this. You'll receive a medal of honor for this, probably the Key to the City."

"You can keep all that, just cut my brother a break. He's a really good man, he just got caught up in trying to do a good thing."

Theresa sighs. "Damn Xavier, I don't know. He's in a lot of shit. I'll see what I can do, but I don't know. He's gonna have to return the money and maybe do some time. But I'll see. I promise you. Cool?"

"Cool." We shake hands as the police car carrying Michael speeds away.

"Well, I need to get back to my team. I still feel I owe you more. Why don't you let me buy you dinner tomorrow?"

"I'd like to, but I think I'm going out with my girlfriend."

"Well, perhaps another time."

"Perhaps."

"I better get going." She reaches in and kisses me on the cheek. "Try to get some sleep, Xavier. Tomorrow is gonna be a long day. I'd need you downtown at 9 A.M."

"All right, I'll see you then."

Heading back to the truck, I stare up at The Savoy and the long line of red and blue lights underneath it. My eyes close, and I thank God for answering my prayers. I get in my truck and sigh, ready to take my tired Black ass home. Frankly, I don't wanna see another TV as long as I live.

AFTERMATH

XAVIER

One year later, Christmas Eve. Man. this is been a crazy year. It's gonna take years for the Feds to figure out all the shit Manning was into. The story is still one of the top pieces on C.N.N. Strangely enough. I still expect to see Theresa on the tube reporting the story.

Speaking of which, Theresa came through big time. Michael turned state's evidence and got immunity from prosecution. The election was held off until May, and Michael won by a landslide. I hope he keeps his nose clean because all eyes are on him, especially Theresa's.

As for me, I'm still Michael's top supporter. Somebody has got to keep him in check. He's already thinking about running for Governor in a couple of years. I saw him and Debra the other day, Christmas shopping at the mall and guess where? Yep freakin' Victoria Secret. I know, I know. I'm scared to ask which one of them they shoppin for?

Kyle is still tryin' to screw everything that moves, but he ain't got to our step-grandmamma Mrs. Jenkins yet. His ass still got jokes after a year. That's all right I'm gonna tell Vanessa's daddy, Fred, where he is if he keeps on.

Jesse sold his house of a 1000 booby traps and Charlie is still livin' in his garage studio with two jogging suits and probably the same pair of draws he left home with. As for me, I'm still dating Gina, no puppies or nothing like that in the works but we holdin' our own.

You know its tripped out. I woke up that day in October last year thinking all I had to worry about was the nookie, but by the end of the night I was a changed man. Life ain't nothing but a state of mind, and when it all goes black the only the thing you leave is that dash on your tombstone between the day you were born and the day you die. You know what, I want it all, I want my dash to be fat, so fat you can see it five miles away over the horizon in London fog. After that day, I don't take anything for granted. I cherish every day, every minute, every single second. So whether I'm 90 with 20 great grandkids or a 90-year old player, it doesn't matter. If the nookie keeps kickin' my ass, day after day, I'm gonna pull off the gloves and savor every round. Peace!